THE BLACK PIT OF TONYPANDY

A novel about the coal mining families
of the Rhondda

The Black Pit of Tonypandy

"If the mines were dangerous places for the men,
the homes were often more dangerous for families."

Myrddin ap Dafydd

translated from the Welsh by Susan Walton

Gwasg Carreg Gwalch

First published in Welsh, *Drws Du yn Nhonypandy*, 2020
Published in English: 2021
© Myrddin ap Dafydd/Carreg Gwalch, 2020
© English translation: Susan Walton, 2020

ISBN: 978-1-84527-829-8

CYNGOR LLYFRAU CYMRU
BOOKS COUNCIL of WALES

Published with the financial support of the Books Council of Wales

Cover design: Eleri Owen
Cover image: Chris Iliff
Maps: Alison Davies

Published by Gwasg Carreg Gwalch,
12 Iard yr Orsaf, Llanrwst, Wales LL26 0EH
tel: 01492 642031
email: books@carreg-gwalch.cymru
website: www.carreg-gwalch.cymru

Printed and published in Wales

This novel was inspired by the community

that developed in Cwm Rhondda

– and the other coal mining areas of Wales –

at a time when the world was demanding

more and more cheap, good-quality coal.

Thanks to Christine James, who was brought up in Tonypandy, for sharing her valuable local knowledge.

Thanks also to Alun Jones, Llio Elenid and Anwen Pierce.

All the Cwm Rhondda characters in this book are fictitious, but there are references to the real historical figures of Mabon (William Abraham), various coal mine owners and Winston Churchill.

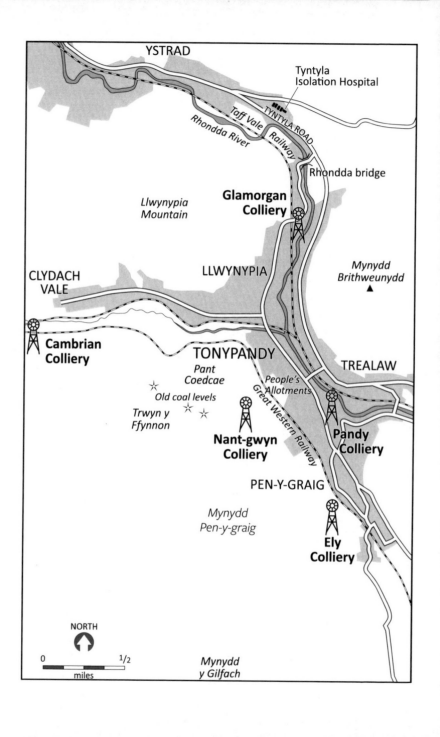

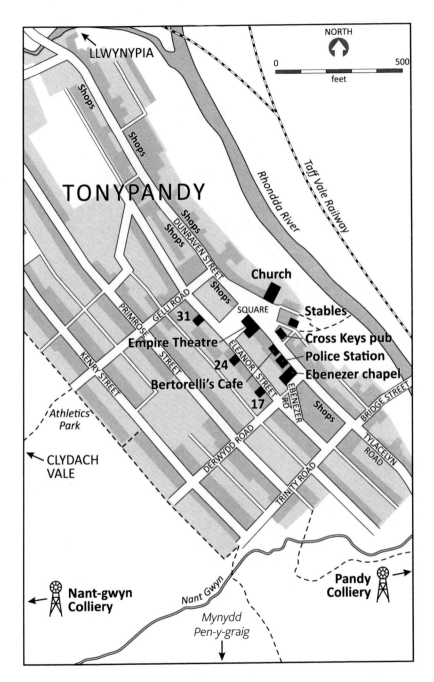

LLWYNYPIA

NORTH

0 500
feet

Shops

Shops

TONYPANDY

Rhondda River

Taff Vale Railway

Shops
DUNRAVEN STREET

Shops

Shops

GELLI ROAD

SQUARE

Church

Stables

31

Empire Theatre

Cross Keys pub

ELEANOR STREET

Police Station

PRIMROSE STREET

24

Ebenezer chapel

Bertorelli's Cafe

EBENEZER RD

KENRY STREET

17

Shops

BRIDGE STREET

Athletics Park

DERWYDD ROAD

TYLACELYN ROAD

CLYDACH VALE

TRINITY ROAD

Nant-gwyn Colliery

Nant Gwyn

Pandy Colliery

Mynydd Pen-y-graig

7

The Families

The Lewis family, Number 17 Eleanor Street, Tonypandy

Guto Lewis   Son; 14 years old; leaving school, and on the point of starting work in the coal mine.

Beti Lewis   Mother; responsible for keeping her family housed, fed, and clean on very little money; pregnant once again.

Moc Lewis   Father; miner in the Glamorgan Colliery, Llwynypia.

Wiliam Lewis   Son; 18 years old; miner in the Glamorgan Colliery, Llwynypia.

Eira Lewis   Daughter; 17 years old; works in a clothing/shoe shop in Tonypandy.

Llew Lewis   Son; 3 years old; a sickly, asthmatic boy.

Dewi Lewis   Son; 18 months old.

Alun the Ox   The lodger at Number 17; 30 years old; a timberman in the Pandy Colliery; a strong, tall man from the Tregaron area of rural mid-Wales.

The Mainwaring family, Number 24 Eleanor Street, Tonypandy

Watcyn Mainwaring — Father; miner in the Pandy Colliery.

Dilys Mainwaring — Mother; responsible for keeping her family housed, fed, and clean on very little money.

Dicw Mainwaring — Son; Guto Lewis's friend.

Edward Mainwaring — Oldest son; miner with his grandfather in the Cambrian Colliery, Clydach Vale.

Sarah Mainwaring — Daughter, 12 years old.

Ann Mainwaring — Daughter; 4 years old.

Emrys Mainwaring — Grandfather; lives in Kenry Street; miner in the Cambrian Colliery, Clydach Vale.

The family at Bertorelli's Cafe

Amadeo (Papà) — Grandfather; owner of Bertorelli's cafe

Pietro Bertorelli — Father; works in the cafe and speaks Welsh and English well.

Emilia Bertorelli — Mother; mostly in the cafe kitchen; cannot speak much Welsh or English.

Nina Bertorelli — Pietro and Emilia's daughter; 13 years old.

Chapter 1

August 1910

Guto Lewis' alarm clock is the sound of feet on the stairs. Those feet are in Number 17, Eleanor Street, Tonypandy in the middle of the valley called Rhondda Fawr.

Flat feet, taking small but quick steps, come first. The same pattern at the same time every morning. At six o'clock, the oil lamp carried by the early riser throws a strip of light under his bedroom door in passing. He hears his mother's arms rubbing against her big apron as she walks downstairs. Swish-swish ...pit-pat ... Spry but full of intent. Guto hears the squeak of the kitchen door as it is opened. Then the metal poker riddling the embers to rekindle the fire. Before long he hears the noise of dry kindling crackling and then his mother putting a shovelful of small coals onto the flames to get some heat going under the water boiler. The thud of the cast iron kettle being placed on the hotplate over the fire comes next.

In his bed, with his eyes closed, Guto can picture his mother busy in the kitchen around which their lives revolve. She was last to bed and before going upstairs at night she would have put the tin bath in the middle of the floor, ready for the end of the night shift. Into it she would have emptied two bucketfuls of cold water. Every mother in the valley learned to put cold water in the bath first, before adding boiling water heated by the open fire in the range. Some years back a small child had died of scalding after falling into boiling bath water. If the mines were dangerous places for the men, the homes were often more dangerous for families. He hears the bucket of coal being emptied onto the fire, now that the flames are taking a proper hold.

He hears the back door opening and his mother going out to the shed to refill the coal bucket. Larger lumps this time, Guto knew. The sort to bring the boiler and the kettle to the boil. His mother comes back in, knocking the doorframe with the bucket because of the weight. He hears the back door close once more.

Things are going well, it seems. He can hear his mother singing a snatch of a song as she reaches for the bread and places it on the table. He hears the cups – already laid on the table – being turned the right way up on their saucers. The sound of water being poured – the teapot is already being warmed.

In the distance, towards Gilfach Road and Llwynypia, Guto hears the sound of hobnailed boots scraping on the flagstones of the street. The first on the day shift are leaving their homes: those who work on the lowest level of the mine. He knows full well what is coming next.

Thud! The house shakes. His father has sprung out of bed and landed squarely on his bedroom floor, both feet together. Then the sound of the chamber pot being pulled out from under the bed and filled. The sound of struggling and mumbling: his father putting on his work trousers and his socks. The bedroom door opening and ...thump-thump! thump-thump! – his father's heavy tread on the stairs, taking them two at a time. The kitchen door opening and closing and voices in the kitchen. There isn't much conversation at this time in the morning. A few words, rather than sentences.

Guto hears his little brother Llew turn in his sleep beside him. Llew has had a fairly quiet night last night. No nasty fits of coughing. But Guto can hear him breathing heavily now, as if there is insufficient air in the room. He can hear his little chest creaking as he fights for breath and then lets it out, then strives immediately to do the same thing again. Guto knows from experience that there would be beads of sweat on his forehead as he exerts himself like this. He feels the quilt being pushed towards him as Llew suddenly flings it away, trying to cool his body. Guto knows that, between him and the wall, Llew *bach* is struggling for air. It is only the end of August, he thinks. Autumn and a long winter are ahead of them.

Further up the valley the harsh screech of the Glamorgan Colliery klaxon at Llwynypia tears through the morning air. Guto knew it was the hooter just after six. That is the first mine in the middle of the valley to call the day shift into the colliery. Five minutes later he hears the Cambrian Colliery hooter at the end of Cwm Clydach. It had to be a calm morning for that one to be heard. It is a few miles up another valley that branches off Rhondda Fawr.

The Glamorgan and the Cambrian, thinks Guto. Two mines but one owner. He's heard a fair amount about that one when his father, his brother and Alun the lodger were sat round the kitchen table discussing colliery life. The hooters of the other mines howl like a pack of wolves hunting among the valley terraces. Ely Colliery, Pen-y-graig – one of the Naval mines would be next to scream, but the same man owned that company too. As Guto emerges from his half-sleep, he suddenly remembers that the Ely Colliery hooter would be silent before long. That mine was shortly to close its gates ...

The sound of hobnailed boots is louder now. Some going to work and some arriving home after the night shift. The odd greeting in the street. Mixed in with this he can hear the occasional clank against a miner's belt of a tin jack for carrying water or tea, as well as metal tommy-boxes – as they call their lunch boxes – knocking against each other in jacket pockets. Guto hears the miners getting closer to Number 17 in the row and then passing by, climbing the steep terraces to their own homes. He imagines the tin bathtubs in every house to welcome them. And the wives, or the landladies of lodging houses, and their pots of tea to warm them before they bathe.

"Wiliam!"

His mother's voice at the foot of the stairs. It is the same every morning. Wiliam is his oldest brother: an eighteen-year-old young man, working at the coalface in the Glamorgan Colliery. But Wiliam likes his bed of a morning. He has a tiny bedroom to himself at the back, but he shares it with the lodger. Shares the bed too – Wiliam sleeps in it at night and Lodger Alun, who works the night shift, sleeps through the daylight hours there. That bed doesn't have time to get cold, thinks Guto – that is going to be lovely in the depths of winter.

"Wiliam! Answer me!"

"Ooo-aaa..." is the attempt at speech from the back bedroom. "Come on, Alun'll need that bed any time now, he will!"

Plonk! Wiliam's two feet hitting the bedroom floor. The smack wasn't as heavy as when his father got up, and this time the building didn't shake.

"Uuurgh ..." The sound of curtains opening and then fumbling. The chamber pot being hosed. More groaning and fumbling – Wiliam is in the midst of his morning battle to find his work clothes. No matter how many times his mother lectures him, thinks Guto, Wiliam never bothers to get his clothes ready in a neat pile for the morning.

He hears his mother open the tap of the boiler, fill the bucket with boiling water and pour it into the bathtub, which is in the middle of the kitchen floor. And then do the same thing again. When Alun arrives through the street door, he will drink his tea and then take off his waistcoat and shirt and wash the grime of the pit off the top half of his body. By now the whole street is ringing to the sound of hobnailed boots.

The next voice to be heard in the house is small and weak. A hesitant little cry to begin with. Silence. Then a longer, stronger cry. Guto knows that Dewi, the baby, eighteen months old, has returned to the world of his bedroom from wherever he'd been wandering in his dreams. Now he won't settle. Another cry.

"Are you going to him, Eira?" Guto whispers across the room.

"Huh? Are you mad?" He hears his sister turn her back on

him in her narrow bed beside the door. It is too early to expect a cheerful response from her.

Dewi continues to cry. Guto hasn't ventured into his parents' bedroom to pick him up since the previous winter. He blamed the gloom of March for that. As he'd been hurrying to Dewi's cradle one of his feet caught the handle of the chamber pot under the bed, which had been sticking out slightly ...

After mopping the floor, Guto had been warned to keep out of his parents' room after that.

Pit-pat, pit-pat. He hears his mother's steps on the stairs. Swift steps again, and with an aim. Bedroom door opening. Then, Dewi's crying stops. His mother rocks him and he hears her singing:

Dafi bach a minne,
Yn mynd i Aberdâr,
Dafi'n mofyn ceiliog,
A minne'n 'mofyn giâr

as they leave the bedroom.

"Wiliam! I'm not telling you again! Alun will be here any minute and it's time for you to get moving!"

The sound of Wiliam's door opening.

That very moment, the Pandy Colliery and Nant-gwyn Colliery hooters sound simultaneously. Those are the worst screeches, being so close to Eleanor Street. Half past six. There is no possibility of going back to sleep once they've disturbed the peace of the morning.

By now the sound of hobnailed boots in the street is going in the other direction. The sound of doors opening and closing up and down the terrace. They have to be down the shaft and at the face by seven o'clock, ready to start cutting coal. He hears his mother going downstairs, lullabying.

He hears his father come through from the kitchen and sit on the bottom stair to lace up his heavy boots. The sound of Wiliam going downstairs, passing his father and then hesitating with the kitchen door ajar. Suddenly he stamps his foot on the stair.

"Ha! One less! I hate to see them, those bloomin' cockroaches!"

He hurries to fetch his jacket from the back.

"Have I got time for a crust of bread?" The sound of tea being gulped down at the same time as putting on his jacket.

"Where on earth is Alun? What do you think, Moc?" he hears his mother call.

"Maybe he's working a double shift," her husband replies. "Dic Tic Toc's his partner and he always seems to be sick." In the mine, every worker has a 'partner' on another shift. If that partner is too ill to come to work, there would be no wage for him and his family. The arrangement between the miners is that the fit partner would work a double shift and give the money from that shift to the sick man's family.

"Where are my boots?" shouts Wiliam, back at the foot of the stairs by now.

"Where's your head, *crwt!*"

The sound of the door again and it's clear that Wiliam has left his boots outside the back door.

"These are still soaking wet!" Wiliam complains yet again.

"Another quarter of an hour and your trousers and shirt will be soaking too!"

Dad's in a grumpy mood, thinks Guto. Then he hears his mother's voice from the kitchen. "This bathwater's getting cold! Where is he?"

He hears the front door opening. The only black door in the street and – in the words of Lodger Alun – "You can't see it at night!"

"Right, we're off, Beti!" calls his father.

"Oh, you take care!" Guto hears the pitter-patter of his mother's feet in the passage. Those are her last words to them every morning. The sound of a kiss on the cheek. "You be careful, Wiliam."

The front door closes. Guto loses track of his father's and brother's footsteps as they join the flow towards the Glamorgan Colliery.

They'll make it to work on time, thinks Guto.

He hears his mother moving the stewpot and putting it over the fire. The smell of supper rises from the kitchen. After his bath, Alun will need his supper before going to bed.

Then his mother comes upstairs again and little Dewi is murmuring happily. She must have wrapped her shawl round him, thinks Guto. He can see it in his mind's eye – the shawl tucked under one of her arms and across the other shoulder. With the little one held contentedly close to his mother's warm body, her hands are free to get on with her work.

Wiliam's bedroom is the focus of her attention now. The sound of the quilt being shaken and the pillow plumped. Then his mother is on her way back. He knows she's carrying the chamber pot. Her pitter-pattering isn't as nimble as usual.

Down the stairs. Sound of the back door. Splash. And then back up the stairs, ready for the lodger.

"Eira! Better think about getting up."

"Ughhhh!" And the sound of a kick under the quilt in the corner.

"You have to have something in your stomach and you have to look tidy to stand in that shop all day!"

Silence.

The sound of hobnailed boots in the street outside has almost faded away into the distance too. No, someone is running past. Someone is going to be late ...

Little Llew is breathing easier by now, and Eira has sunk back into sleep.

Guto gets up and dresses before venturing downstairs in his stockinged feet with a light and careful step. He quietly pushes open the kitchen door. He sees his mother sitting at the kitchen table with her hand round a cup of tea. Her other arm holds Dewi, sitting astride her hip, his eyes wide awake and his curls bouncing in a halo round his smiling face on seeing his brother.

"Well, good morning, monkey!" Guto makes animal noises and pretends to chew the ear of the little one. "Would you like me to give Dewi his breakfast, Mam?"

Beti Lewis had been lost in thought when he spoke. She jumps, putting her hand to her belly in fright. Guto looks at the swell of her pregnancy with concern.

"Are you alright, Mam? Is the baby alright? Is it starting ...?"

"No, no, *crwtyn*, don't fuss," answers his mother.

"Nothing's wrong. It won't be coming for another three months yet."

"Let me take little Dewi!" Guto smiles at him.

Beti Lewis accepts his offer, and places Dewi in his waiting arms.

"Shall we play chase, big man?" Guto lowers the toddler onto the floor and starts to run after him.

"Not round the hot bath!" shouts their mother. "And don't you get your socks wet – the floor's wet round the tub."

Guto opens the door to the passage, shepherding Dewi past him to carry on playing out there.

That's when they hear the sound of hobnailed boots. Boots coming towards Eleanor Street from the colliery. Boots walking slowly and carefully. As if carrying something ... or somebody ...

Beti Lewis stands, leaving her cup on the table.

"Oh no!" she says. "Something's happened at the pit ..."

Chapter 2

Guto and his mother, Beti Lewis, stand behind the closed front door, both holding their breath. They hear the hobnailed boots marching slowly, getting closer. The occasional nail scrapes the stone surface of the road and the sound goes through them. The boots have reached Number 17 ... And then ... the group passes by. Guto's mother lets out a sigh of relief.

"Not our house this time," she says.

Guto looks at her silently.

"I know," she says, opening the door and stepping out onto the doorstep. "They're going to someone else's home. I hope he's not hurt too badly ..."

Standing at the top of the steps that lead from the street up to the front door, they can see the backs of the miners going onwards up the street. Six of them are carrying a wooden frame supporting a sheet of canvas. On the canvas is a shape, covered with a blanket, but the blanket had not been pulled up to hide the head.

"He's been injured, *bach*," says Beti Lewis. "Too badly to walk, too, poor thing."

Guto looks back down in the direction of the Pandy Colliery. Every door in the terrace has been opened and in all the doorways concerned families are gathered to hear the bad news. He turns back to the rescue party. Holding the back of the stretcher is Alun, their lodger; he can pick him out because he's three or four inches taller than any other miner in the street.

Guto realises that the miners are standing in the street and that one of them has ascended the steps to the door of a house in their terrace.

"Dilys Mainwaring, Number 24!" exclaims Beti. "It's Watcyn, poor thing!"

Before the miner can knock, the door opens wide.

Guto can see Dilys standing there – her back straight and her jaw set. She's ready to hear the worst.

By now the women and some of the children have left their own doorsteps and have gathered round the miners, the injured man and Number 24. Guto hears the miner at the door telling Dilys Mainwaring what has happened.

"It happened two hours ago. We'd almost finished the night shift, too. Watcyn was here, and Jerry Bach, his butty, was heaving coal away from the face ... Jerry Bach was heaving the big lumps onto the tram and Watcyn's at the face with his mandrel ... And a bang from somewhere and down comes a rock from the roof ... Broke through the pit props like they were paper ... Half a ton of rock on top of Jerry Bach and then Watcyn ... He got whacked on the back of the head, did Watcyn ... There was no hope for Jerry Bach, poor thing."

The miner turns and nods towards the man lying on the stretcher. He hasn't moved a muscle.

"Bring him up the steps, boys. Careful, now ..."

"How ... How is he?" Dilys asks.

"He's reasonably comfortable, I think," answers one of

the miners. "The doctor came to the pithead. He's given him something to make him sleep. He needs rest and sleep now. His head's had a hard knock, you see."

As the miners negotiate the steps, Guto can see a bandage round Watcyn Mainwaring's head. Around both sides of the back of his head, the red has spread, staining the bandage.

The stretcher party goes into the house, leaving the door open. Gradually the little crowd disperses back their own houses, murmuring.

"Jerry Bach – I know his mother."

"He's Watcyn's younger brother's son, you see."

"Over on the road to Cwm Clydach, they live, don't they."

"Yes, that's right. 'Ee'd only jus' started in the pit las' Jan'ry, 'ee 'ad."

"Oh, dear, dear ... How unfortunate for them."

"And unfortunate for the Mainwarings too. They don't have a lodger, or anyone to bring any money in now ..."

"There's some misfortune every week in this valley."

Back in the kitchen, Guto and his mother exchange very few words. Beti Lewis has tipped another bucketful of hot water into the bath. Before she can go out the back once more, Guto takes the bucket from her and goes out to the tap in the gully – the back lane behind the house. By the time he comes back into the kitchen, Lodger Alun is sitting on his haunches in front of the range.

"The rock's so uneven in the Rhondda, isn't it," he says. "It's a devil of a thing. Sometimes the grain is going with you. Then suddenly it's all upended. You've got a wonderful little seam of the best steam coal in the world – and suddenly it disappears under a lump of useless rock that's been pushed over it. It's difficult to work here. But worse than being difficult – it's so dangerous."

Guto empties the bucket of water into the boiler. His mother will need more hot water to wash clothes before long.

"How bad is Watcyn, then?" asks Beti.

"Don't ask. He's lost a bit of his skull at the back. You can see his—"

"That's enough for now, Alun," says Beti, glancing at Guto. "Can you go into the pantry and fetch me an egg for your breakfast, *gw'boi*. Are you going to start your wash, Alun?"

Alun stands up from where he is squatting, and in so doing cracks his head on the high mantleshelf above the fire.

"Ouch! I forgot about that!"

He unwinds his muffler from round his neck, and then takes off his jacket and his waistcoat and places them all to dry on the wooden drying rack hanging above the fire. Before long, steam rises from them, creating damp clouds in the kitchen.

He pulls off his flannel shirt and tosses it in a wet and filthy heap in the corner. He gets down on all fours in front of the bathtub, leans over it, and submerges his head in the water.

"Is it warm enough? It's been standing a while," says Beti, when he raises his head of blond hair out of the water once more. Dewi laughs uproariously when Alun shakes his head, showering him with drops of water.

"Yes, it's fine. Good enough to rinse this muck off."

Alun spends a few minutes carefully washing his eyes. Every underground worker sets great store by this. Very often their eyes are bloodshot when they leave the pit. The coal dust irritates them and the poor light from their lamps they have to work by strains their eyesight.

When he's finished, Beti passes him the carbolic soap and he begins by soaping his arms and front and washing his hair.

"Ready?" asks Beti, once most of his upper body is pink once more.

Without replying, Alun leans forward as far as he can over the bathtub, supporting himself with his hands, so that his shoulders and as much as possible of his back are above the water. Then Beti takes the soap and starts rubbing it over his shoulders and back so that the suds work the coal dust off.

Guto never tires of marvelling at this process. The coal mines down the valley are worked in shafts hundreds of feet underground. That is where the seams of coal are found and it's a great challenge to go so far into the earth to hew the coal and bring it to the surface to feed the insatiable worldwide demand of ship and train engines.

Because they are such deep pits, they are incredibly hot and the miners often work half-naked. It's a job to wash off the combination of sweat and coal dust at the end of each shift.

Now and again Alun flinches as Beti washes his back.

"Another cut, is it?" she says, spotting a scrape or cut on his flesh.

As the blackness is washed off his body, Guto can see the blue lines of past scars and the new, red injuries from recent shifts. There is no time for the injuries to heal properly before the next shift, so by the time they do heal they will have closed over coal dust which stays under the skin, giving the scar its distinctive hue.

"You'll have make the roof of the tunnel higher, Alun – your back's all ridged with scars; it looks like a potato field!"

"It's the Rhondda colliers' fault: they're so short, Bet!" he retorts. "I swear they only need about two foot of tunnel, they do. They've not made the roof high enough for a country boy like me."

"It's you that's a great ox of a Cardi and not used to being a mole," replies Beti.

Alun is a 'Cardi' – from Ceredigion. His official name is Alun Jones, but he's Alun the Ox in Tonypandy. The mining families of the Valleys tend to be short and dark-complexioned, but Alun is of a different breed, and he has just come back from six weeks' work on the harvest back home.

"What do they feed you with in the countryside? You're as sleek as a bullock!"

"Harvest home supper every night, you know!" Alun says. "And none of your one-egg-for-breakfast lark – they feed you about half a pig!"

"Well, don't you be expecting that here on the money I get from you as a lodger!"

Beti straightens up and lets out a little sigh as she massages the base of her back with her fist.

"Not long to go now, Beti," says Alun, as he stands up, takes off his trousers and puts them on over the fireguard. In no time at all he is sitting in the bath, stark naked, washing the rest of his body.

"Do you know what, Guto," he says, turning his head towards the boy, "some colliers refuse to wash their backs. They leave the coal dust there, and say it makes their backs stronger!"

"I saw them on the beach at Porthcawl last year," Guto says. "A row of black backs!"

"Imagine if I went home and took off my shirt to carry hay looking like that! They'd laugh at me and call me a Welsh Black bull." He play-acts two horns and makes a bellowing sound, much to the amusement of Dewi, who is holding onto the edge of the bath.

Beti opens the door to the passage to give Eira another shout, before picking up Alun's trousers and putting them on the drying rack. She picks up his underclothes and shirt and carries them out to the wooden washing tub out the back.

"How was little Llew this morning?" Alun asks Guto.

"No better."

"Right, bring me that egg," says Beti on her return. She drains a little water from the boiler into a saucepan and puts the egg into it, over the fire. She gives the stewpot a stir and hands Alun, who is still relaxing in the bath, a bowlful. She lifts the baby up from the floor and holds him on her lap to spoon-feed him and then passes him to Guto and eats some bread herself.

It is gone eight o'clock when Eira appears downstairs.

"Do you want some of this?" says Guto, proffering the egg to Dewi. But he shakes his head and turns away.

"Come on now, my blue-eyed boy," says Alun from the bath. "'*O din iâr i'th gadw'n iach*' is what my Uncle Ned Ffair-rhos says about eggs – eat up!"

Eira wrinkles her nose as she looks into the saucepan on the table.

"No egg for me, then?" she asks curtly.

"It's too late now," her mother replies. "You'd better shake a leg if you're going to get to that shop on time."

"It's only round the corner, Mam!" the girl protests. "I'll get a sausage roll from Bracchi's down the street, I will."

"Where did you get those new shoes?" exclaims Beti.

"From Mr Davies! They're proper ladies' shoes for working in the shop. I'm fed up of wearing boots. Special staff price on the summer stock. He's taking threepence from my wages every week."

"It's a wonder you've got any actual wages, you've got so much on the never-never," her mother comments drily.

"*Jiw-jiw*, Mam, everyone in the valley's on the never-never these days."

"Mister Elias Davies, Ladies' Outfitter and Draper, that's him, isn't it?" says Alun from the bath. "He must be rubbing his hands together thinking of what he'll sell this autumn, now he's got rid of his summer dresses."

"Ooo, Alun," says Eira in feigned shock. "I didn't know that you were interested in women's clothes!"

"No, I'm interested in Elias Davies."

"Of course!" replies the girl. "Ebenezer chapel folk stick together, don't they! And he's a Cardi as well, isn't he?"

"No, he's the son of a Cardi," says Alun lightly, getting out of the bath and grabbing a towel hanging over the back of one of the chairs.

He reaches for a dry flannel shirt and long johns from the pile airing above the fire.

"Come over to the table to finish your supper," says Beti, gesturing to his half-eaten bowl of meat and potato stew.

Supper and then to bed for the rest of the day was the pattern for Alun. He had to be down on the level and ready for work as a colliery timberman by ten at night, so he needs to leave the house a few minutes after nine. Like many of the lads from west Wales who are in the pits, he can handle an axe, a saw and a sledgehammer. The Rhondda collieries needs good timbermen to construct and position the pit props to support the roofs of the underground tunnels.

"Eira, could you take this pot of bramble jam to the Mainwarings on your way?" says her mother, fetching a jar from the pantry.

"I don't have time, Mam! I've got to go."

"I'll take it up to them," says Guto.

Beti Lewis disappears upstairs to check on Llew. When she returns to the kitchen, Guto is busy with a bucket, scooping up the bathwater and carrying it out the back.

Chapter 3

This time, it is Moc Lewis sitting in the bath and Wiliam, his son, who is sitting on his haunches beside the fire. Dewi's little hand is splashing in the bathwater.

"*Ych-a-fi*, Dewi!" says his mother as she passes him to put potatoes in the supper stewpot. "That's dirty water. Dirty! D'you understand?"

The wide smile on the face of the toddler showed he wasn't at all bothered by the coal dust clouding the water.

"Moc, love, could you keep an eye on the little one while I'm out the back?"

"What do you mean, woman? I'm starkers and in the bath!"

"Will Mabon be at the meeting tonight, then, Dad?" asks Wiliam.

"I'm not sure he'll make it," Moc answers. "He's a member of parliament in London now, you know. And he has a lot of important things to attend to ..."

"There's important things in Cwm Rhondda too!"

"I know that, son. But you must remember that there's a weight on his shoulders ..."

"There's a weight on his belly too. My goodness, he's as fat as the pit owner."

"Give him his due, now. He's worked hard for the Fed, fair play. If it hadn't been for Mabon, there wouldn't be a Fed for us."

The conversation lapses for a while. Moc thinks about the trials and tribulations of the twelve years since the South Wales Miners' Federation had been created. That was the Fed – the workers' union – and Mabon is its leader. He is a bear-like figure, with a voice like a bull. He could get a crowd singing hymns in powerful unison when some of the workers' meetings get too heated. By now he is the Labour Member of Parliament for Rhondda.

Beti comes back into the kitchen.

"Moc, can you fill a bucket of coal for me?"

"I can't just now, woman! I'm naked and I haven't dried myself yet!"

Moc continues his pondering. "Yes, in unity there is strength. And Mabon has given the miners strength for a quarter of a century."

"Maybe it's time to think about the next quarter of a century now, Dad. The pit owners had their own union a quarter of a century before the Fed!" Wiliam says bitterly.

"The rock is tricky in the Rhondda, but the masters want the same tonnage of coal from every level in every pit," says Moc. "It's just not possible."

"And the biggest master of them all – David Thomas – is offering us a low price per ton as well. That's the bone of contention in the Ely pit."

"Yes. Every time a new level is opened in one of the pits, the price per ton they offer us falls. We don't know where we stand."

"Stand?" The door opens and Alun walks in. He's obviously been out for a walk after his sleep. "Better not stand up in the bath, Moc, or Beti will complain that there's water all over the floor."

"But it is time for you to get out, Dad," says Wiliam, "or the water'll be too cold for me to wash properly."

Moc eases himself upwards and starts drying himself. Wiliam takes off his flannel shirt and before long they have swapped places.

"I'll wash his back, Beti," says Alun, seeing the housewife hurrying in from the back. "You carry on with what you need to do."

"Your best shirt's been ironed and it's on the rail above the fire," Beti tells her husband. "You'll need it for the meeting tonight. Give me those wet trousers, Wiliam. I'll put them to dry on the fireguard."

Wiliam finishes undressing and Beti takes the two miners' clothes out to the wooden wash tub in the back yard. Seconds later she's back for a bucketful of hot water from the boiler to wash them and scrub the coal dust out of them.

"Earlier on, when I said 'stand', I meant I don't know where we stand with our wages," Moc explained to Alun once he was settled in his chair. "Fixed wages and fixed hours."

"Too right," Alun says. "I wouldn't have bothered coming all the way to Tonypandy from the Tregaron countryside if I didn't know how much money I'd be taking home."

"And eight hours underground," added Moc. "The Fed under Mabon got us that too. When my dad was young, he worked twelve hours a day in the pit in Merthyr."

"But fewer hours means less coal as well, remember, Moc," Alun says.

"But these pits are bringing up more coal now than ever!" Wiliam insists, as Alun rinses the soap off his back.

"In you hop now!" says Alun. "Yes, yes – the world is crying out for Rhondda coal. The best steam coal – that's what's in the rocks beneath us, boys. And half of it's in this here bathtub, I can tell you!"

Alun sits down on his haunches beside the fireplace. Having settled himself in the tub, Wiliam resumes the discussion.

"And that's why tonight's meeting is so important. What the owners are doing now is chipping away at our wages. Yes, yes – we have a guaranteed wage. But they're knocking bits off morning, noon and night, they are."

"You're right," answers Alun. "I've got a new axe to trim the props in the tunnels – but I had to pay for it myself."

"And you'll have to pay to sharpen it too," adds Moc. "It's us who buys every tool we use at the face, it is."

"And then we have to buy the powder to put into the blast holes," Wiliam says. "And now they're trying to reduce the minimum wage still further."

"They don't trust us, see," Moc says. "They think that paying us per shift would mean the miners would be slower and bring up less coal."

"They don't understand the mines," says Wiliam. "The rock is difficult in the Rhondda, it is. It's difficult to reach the seams – sometimes we have to dig out so much rock to reach the coal and sometimes the seam is useless anyway, and it wasn't worth the effort."

"That's why the Ely pit lads are meeting in the Empire

tonight, isn't it boys," Alun says. "Are you Glamorgan boys coming too, to support us?"

"Of course we are, mun. I'm going upstairs to finish dressing and I'll pop over to see the Mainwarings before supper," Moc says.

"Only one shilling and ninepence for a day's shift cutting coal!" scoffs Wiliam from the lukewarm bathwater. "That's all they're offering the Ely colliers! I know that the Ely is owned by the Naval Company, and that we're owned by the Cambrian Company – but they might as well be the same thing. The same master owns the two. The pittance that's being offered at the Ely'll be offered to us very soon."

"And even less for the timbermen who keep the tunnels safe," Alun adds.

"The worries are different for each of you," says Beti, carrying more coal for the fire. "Do you have to get so much water on the floor, *crwt*?"

"Dad made those splashes!" says Wiliam. "Everyone else gets a shower when he's drying himself."

"And I might as well ask this bucket to clear up after itself as ask him to." She storms off out the back.

"How many'll be at the Empire tonight, then?" Alun asks.

"The place holds over five hundred, I reckon," answers Wiliam. "The it'll be packed, you'll see."

The Empire was one of Tonypandy's biggest theatres on Dunraven Street – the main street. On special evenings the film projectors are stilled so that the miners can hold their meetings. A new coal seam at the Ely Colliery, Pen-y-graig, is the subject under discussion that evening. The seam has been opened and worked by eighty colliers for a trial period so that the owners can measure the output and calculate the daily wage to be offered to the workers.

The output has been disappointing.

The rock was difficult to work, said the miners.

We cannot offer more than one shilling and ninepence a day, said the owners.

The lowest wage in Britain! said the Ely miners contemptuously.

That's your fault, for deliberately working slowly during the trial period, said the owners.

We'll accept nothing less than half a crown a day, said the workers. That's two shillings and sixpence a day, or there will be no coal cut at the Ely.

In that case, said the owners, no one will work the coal there. We're closing the pit. From Thursday the first of September no one will be working – or receiving wages – in the Ely Colliery.

A lockout! said the miners. You close the gates to the colliery and there'll be eight hundred of us left with no wage.

One shilling and ninepence a day or nothing, said the owners.

Half a crown a day or nothing!

As Wiliam is pondering the situation, the front door opens and closes and Guto comes into the kitchen.

"Is it true, Wil?" he asks his brother, who by now is out of the bath and drying himself.

"Is what true, for goodness' sake?"

"Dicw just told me."

"And what did Dicw just tell you?" Dicw is one of the Mainwarings' sons. He is the same age and in the same class as Guto.

"That one collier gets killed at work every week in Cwm Rhondda."

"Well, yes, the number must be pretty high. And how's Watcyn Mainwaring?"

"Still sleeping. Dilys Mainwaring is at his bedside. She's been moistening his lips with a cloth and a bowl of water all day. But he hasn't stirred."

"Is Edward back from his shift?"

Contrary to the usual pattern, the oldest Mainwaring son does not work in the same pit as his father. He clears coal for his grandfather, Emrys Mainwaring, at the face in the Cambrian Pit in Cwm Clydach. His grandfather hacks out the big pieces of coal from the seam, and his grandson – his 'butty *bach*' – loads these big pieces onto the tram. They are then pulled along the rails to the bottom of the shaft, and from there lifted up to the surface.

"Yes, he came home as usual."

"Had he heard?"

"Not at work, but Dicw and I were waiting for him when he came up to the surface in the cage."

"And how are little Ann and Sarah?" Alun asks from his seat in the corner.

"Sarah's making supper and Ann was holding the towel for her brother while he was having a bath."

"How old are they now?"

"Sarah's two years younger than Dicw and me. Twelve. And Ann – she's about four."

"They lost two boys between those two, didn't they?"

"I've seen their gravestone in Trealaw cemetery," Guto says. "I went over there in the summer with Dicw and we picked flowers and took them there."

"Have you had tea, Guto?" asks Beti, starting to empty the bath with a bucket.

"I'll do that, Mam," answers Guto, taking the heavy bucket out of her hand. "I had bread and jam with Sarah Mainwaring."

"You don't eat at their house at a time like this, d'you understand?" scolded Beti.

"But it was our jar of bramble jam, Mam!"

"I gave the jam to them – not for you to go there and fill your own stomach."

It took four journeys with the water for Guto to empty the bath. There were several more pools of water on the stone floor by now, as Dewi, clutching the back of a chair, had been stamping his little feet in one of the puddles.

Moc Lewis comes back downstairs, dressed in his waistcoat and black trousers, and with the chain of his a pocket watch hanging across the front of his waistcoat. He sits down in the most comfortable chair in the room and picks up the newspaper.

Seeing Dewi dancing in the puddle, Beti picks him up and puts him on his father's knee. He starts pulling at Moc's paper.

"Can't I have a bit of peace, woman?"

"Well, if you don't want Dewi on your lap, can you help Guto take this bath out?"

"I'm in my best clothes!"

"Did you look in on little Llew while you were upstairs?"

"I didn't know he was in bed. It was quiet, in any case."

"He's been in bed all day." Beti goes out the back to fill a bowl of water and carry it upstairs.

Moc closes his paper, stands up and plops Dewi back down on the wet floor.

"I'm going to the Institute before supper," he calls to Beti.

"Don't go wandering too long," she shouts back from half way up the stairs.

"I'm going out for a shave before we eat," Alun says. The others hear the familiar bang as his head hits the mantleshelf and the items on it rock. "Ouch! Does this have to be here?"

"Where else can we put clothes that have been ironed? And while you're outside, go and tell those kids playing ball in the street to stay away from Number 24. They need a bit of peace."

"Why don't you come with me to the Institute on Saturday afternoon?" Alun invites Guto as he heads for the door.

"Pah!" scoffs Beti. "The Institute's a place for men to escape to out of earshot of their wives when they need help at home!"

"There's more to it than that," Alun says. "You can go to the library and borrow a book. It's all free. Or to the reading room to read the newspapers and see what's happening in the big wide world. I could teach you a trick or two on the snooker table."

Guto remembers the first time he went to the Workmen's Hall and Institute with Alun. The weather was too wet to be outside and there was nothing much else to do. He'd felt quite grown up going into this men's sanctum. He had quickly noticed that many of the men there were very old. Or at least looked very old. Their faces were drawn and they were short of breath. He saw one man with his arm in a sling, and another on crutches. These were men who could no longer work.

He'd found the reading room extremely interesting. Alun showed him the different newspapers and periodicals, explaining the differences between them. He'd read column after column of print. After this experience, he would return regularly to this room in the Institute.

Chapter 4

"Hey! What are you doing with your hand in the jug?"

Guto enters the kitchen without warning after clearing
the supper plates. Alun has put on his work clothes ready for
his night shift and gone out for a breath of fresh air to the
main street before going to the meeting in the Empire. Wil
has gone to the bar of the Cross Keys Hotel on Dunraven
Street to wet his whistle with a gang of the younger miners
before the meeting. Beti is upstairs with Llew and Dewi.

The kitchen is seldom so empty. Eira is standing in front
of the fire. She has lifted a white jug down from the high
mantleshelf. Guto has caught her with her hand in the jug.

"That's Mam's money. What are you doing with it?"

Eira doesn't turn a hair. She pulls her hand out and looks
at the coins she's holding.

"There we are," she says. "A penny for the sausage roll for
breakfast and a penny ha'penny for the frothy coffee and
sandwich at lunch time."

She tips the rest of the money back into the jug and
places it back on the shelf.

"Have you had permission from Mam to do that?"

"It's money for food for the household, isn't it? Well,
that's my breakfast and lunch. You had an egg for breakfast, I
had breakfast and lunch in Bracchi's."

"But you could have had your breakfast here and taken a

packed lunch with you if you'd got up early enough!"

"What do you know, *gw'boi*? What do you know about working? Out of the way. It's none of your business, anyhow."

She slams the front door behind her and walks out into the street.

Guto climbs the stairs and joins his mother in the bedroom.

"Oh, look, Llew love," Beti says. "Guto's come to see how you are."

Beti is sitting in the middle of the bed with Llew leaning against one side, his head on her breast. Beti's hand is on his forehead. At her other side Dewi is cuddled up. At last he's quiet and his eyes are drowsy.

"You're coughing less now, Llew," Guto says.

"He's worse at night, aren't you, *bach*?" says his mother. "But maybe the onion will help tonight. I boiled a whole onion for him, you see, Guto. From the string of onions I got from the Johnny Onions the other day. They're good onions. A good strong smell on them. And they're pinkish inside. It's because they use seaweed on the fields, they say. Anyway, they're good for asthma and clearing the chest. That's what Mam would tell us children. Boil the onion in milk and eat it with a bit of vinegar and brown sugar. You enjoyed that, didn't you, *bach*?"

Llew murmurs his contentment and closes his eyes once more.

"We sang at school today, Llew," says Guto. "Miss Humphreys is good at finding new songs for us. She had some sort of magazine with a red cover and inside there was a song about the stagecoach ..."

"Tell Llew what a stagecoach is, Guto."

"Well, a long time ago, before steam trains and tramcars and the modern things we travel in today, people went on journeys in a coach with big wheels and four or six horses to pull it. Can you believe that? No engine, no firebox or coal – nothing but horses! There was a picture of the coach and people in the clothes of the time and the horses in Miss Humphreys' magazine."

"Do you remember the song, then, Guto?"

"The chorus went like this:

Yn Nyddiau'r Hen Goets Fawr, yn Nyddiau'r Hen Goets Fawr;
Mae hiraeth ar fy nghalon am Ddyddiau'r Hen Goets Fawr."

"Lovely, Guto! That's easy enough to remember, isn't it, Llew my love? You sing the verse, Guto, and we'll join in the chorus, shall we, Llew?"

"The first verse went like this:

Mae'r oes yn rhuthro'n gyflym, nad ŵyr hi ddim i b'le,
Mewn brys a rhuthr ofnadwy, ar gefn mellt y ne'!
Yng nghanol twrf peiriannau, hiraethaf lawer awr
Am roddi llam, a disgyn yn Nyddiau'r Hen Goets Fawr."

Beti joins in on the chorus, rocking the two little boys from side to side.

"Can you remember another verse, Guto?"

"Oh, there were over twenty verses in the song! But I remember this one:

Roedd ganddynt fwy o hamdden, er gweithio'n ddiwyd iawn,
I sylwi ac i feddwl o fore hyd brynhawn;
A chysgent a breuddwydient drwy'r nos hyd doriad gwawr
Yn llawer iawn mwy melys yn Nyddiau'r Hen Goets Fawr."

"Oh, true enough!" Beti says.

"Yn Nyddiau'r Hen Goets Fawr, yn Nyddiau'r Hen Goets Fawr;
Mae hiraeth ar fy nghalon am Ddyddiau'r Hen Goets Fawr."

"What a good song, and well done for remembering it, Guto," says his mother. "It takes us back to an earlier time, doesn't it? And there's something to be said for those times, rather than scrabbling here for work and wages and destroying the earth and creating waste tips everywhere. This valley's turning the same colour as the coal – but it was clean and full of nature fifty years ago. Honestly, what are we doing?"

Quietly, without moving his lips, Llew is humming the chorus.

"You're starting to learn it, Llew!" says his brother. "You'll know it all properly before you start school. When can he go to nursery school, Mam?"

"He'll be four in January. He can go then."

"He's more than ten years younger than me, isn't he, Mam?"

"Yes."

"You once said there had been other children between me and him, didn't you?"

"But it wasn't meant to be, Guto."

"Brothers or sisters?"

"One of each. We lost one in the womb. A little girl. She was stillborn. She would have been ten by now."

"Oh, and I would have had a little sister, Mam."

"And then Bobi came into the world. But he wasn't with us long. He was six months old when he got dysentery. He couldn't keep anything inside. Dirty drinking water, the doctor said."

"Why haven't I seen their graves in Trealaw cemetery, Mam?"

"Well, their graves are there. They're buried together. But there's no headstone yet. A stone is expensive, you see. And the living need money more than the dead."

Guto looks at Llew for a long time.

"Wouldn't it be better for us to get the doctor to take a look at him, Mam?"

"Doctors are expensive too, Guto. They can charge two shillings just for coming through the door. And then there's the cost of medicine on top of that."

"But Mam, there's enough money in the jug, isn't there? Dad puts money in, and Wil. Lodger Alun puts money for food and rent in the jug."

"Yes, between them all we're alright."

"And Eira puts money in the jug too, doesn't she?"

Another silence falls between them.

"Right," says his mother, lifting Llew's head and placing it gently on the pillow. "These boys are ready to go to sleep."

She gathers Dewi into her arms and stands up. Dewi had

been sucking his thumb for a while and is ready to settle for the night. This mother starts to carry him through to their bedroom.

She turns in the doorway and sees Guto about to kiss Llew good night.

"Guto! No, best not to. Don't you remember me saying?"

"What?"

"You could infect Llew just by kissing him. His chest is too weak for you to chance it."

"But I'm not poorly, Mam. I'm as fit as a fiddle."

"You can carry an infection without knowing about it. That's how these horrible diseases are passed on so quickly, and we're all living on top of each other in this valley."

Back down in the kitchen, his mother says to Guto, "Why don't you go round to Dicw Mainwaring's? He could do with a bit of a change and to get out of the house. Are you going to the Empire? You've got an hour before it starts."

"Are youngsters like us allowed?"

"You can't vote, of course – only members of the Fed can do that. But there'll be a lot of miners' children there."

"Does anything else need doing here?"

"Oh, I'll be alright. Just laying the table for breakfast."

"And filling the boiler and carrying coal in – do you want me to do that?"

"No, I'll manage. Your place is with Dicw – and give them my regards."

Before long the two lads are walking down Eleanor Street in the direction of the Pandy Colliery and then along Dunraven Street. The street is bustling because of the big meeting. Great tramcars run down the middle of the street from Pen-y-graig. These are overflowing with miners in their best clothes and flat caps. Many of the shops have remained open to make the most of the crowd.

As they stroll down the long street, there are plenty of delicious foods and enticing produce to take their fancy.

"Oh! Look at this chocolate, Dicw! I could lie in this window all day and eat the bloomin' lot!"

"Well, I've got bottles of pop here in Morgan's. Look! Cherryade, dandelion and burdock, and even limeade! All from the Welsh Hills Mineral factory down in Porth, so they say! Have you tasted it?"

"Yes, our lodger, Alun the Ox, brought some cherryade for us once. It tickles your nose and makes you belch – but the taste is amazing!"

They walk past a shop window filled with fruit, some of which they can't even name. A butcher's shop, a furniture shop ... The people of the valley must be buying this stuff ...

The pair cross the side street that climbs at an angle past Ebenezer chapel and its vestry, then they pass the police station – where three policemen are standing, keeping a keen eye on the crowd – before the shops start again.

"This is where your sister works, isn't it, Guto?"

They are looking into the window of Elias Davies Ladies' Outfitter and Draper by now.

"Oh, Mam would look so posh in that hat over there," says Dicw. "Look! There's half a cemetery's worth of flowers on it!"

"And what about those stylish gloves here?" Guto adds.

"Just the job for carrying the coal bucket, aren't they?"

"This shop's closed, Guto."

"Yes. They're not likely to sell much to a bunch of colliers. Maybe their daughters come here, wanting to look like the smart wives and daughters of the bosses."

They hear a sudden rap on a window. They are passing Bertorelli's cafe and none other than Lodger Alun and his partner Dic Tic Toc are seated at the window table. Alun gestures to them to come inside.

Once they are inside, they marvel at the place. Guto has been there twice before, and had been bewitched by the sumptuousness of everything. The wood of the counter has a high polish, the till shines, the glass cake stands are bright and clean, and every jar and tin and piece of crockery and the weighing scales sparkle.

Behind the counter are two men. One is about the same age as the boys' fathers. He is slim, with an olive skin, and wearing a tidy white shopkeeper's dustcoat. Every hair on his head is in place and every one of them shines with some sort of oil. A white shirt and collar and a black tie. He hurries back and forth, dealing with customers with a smile, and turning every so often to the shiny coffee machine behind him to conjure into being – with a mixture of roaring and steam – the cups of coffee.

At the far end of the counter, near the door through to the back, an old boy stands. The slim man's father. His arms are folded and he sits back with his behind on a shelf. But his eyes are like a hawk's, darting round the cafe and observing what is going on at every table. He raises an occasional finger to his son, nods towards a particular table and says a few words the lads don't understand. But the son understands – he will come out from behind the counter then and clear the dirty pots that have been brought to his attention. Then it's out through to the back with the dirty crockery.

"Well, how are the young men tonight, then?" Alun asks when the two lads come over to his table. "Out chasing girls, is it?"

They are both about to protest loudly at such a stupid idea when Alun smiles and nods towards the empty chairs.

"Sit down here, what would you like? Tea? Frothy coffee? Pop?"

"Pop, please, Alun. May I have the red one, the cherryade?"

"And what colour would you like, Mainwaring?"

"I'll have the dark one. The burdock."

"Okey-doke. Sit tight. I'll be two minutes."

Guto sees the man behind the counter take Alun's order at once. A cheery wave of his arms, a friendly laugh and in no time at all Alun places two glasses of pop in front of them, the change in his hand.

"This is what's nice about these Italian cafes: they're in no rush to get you to leave the table, you see," Alun says as he places the glasses in front of the boys. "Isn't that splendid? Yes, indeed. You can end up staying all evening if you want. They're so congenial and there's no rush. They'll still be open after the meeting at the Empire, you'll see."

"They're talking the language of Italy to each other, are they?" Guto asks, after taking a slurp of his pop.

"Oh yes, they all speak Italian. There are a lot of them in this valley. They all come from one town in Italy – one person came here originally, then his brother and his cousin and then neighbours of his brother – and now there are two or three cafes in every village in the Rhondda. Bertorelli is the name of this family here."

"And who are the two lads, Aluno Jose?" The tall, slim man has just cleared the table behind them and has stopped for a moment to exchange a few words as he passes their table.

"Two lads! We have two young men here, Pietro," Alun replies. "This is Guto, the son of the house where I lodge, and his partner, Dicw Mainwaring. Boys, this is Pietro Bertorelli, one of the men from the best cafe in the Rhondda."

"How old are you, Guto and Dicw?" Pietro is taking a great interest in the two lads.

"Fourteen," answers Guto.

"A good age! *Bene, bene,*" smiles Pietro. "Is the pop nice?"

"Yes, very nice, thank you."

"*Bene, bene!*" And off he goes with a pile of crockery.

"Hey! Drink up!" Alun says. "We'll have to get a move on to get into the Empire."

"Yes, the clock is ticking," says Dic Tic Toc.

Chapter 5

There is a huge audience in the Empire and the place is full of light. There is an electricity supply to most of the businesses on the main street of Tonypandy by now, and there are electric streetlights along the street, and even along some of the side streets. Every mine has its own powerhouse to provide electricity to pump out water from the lowest levels – essential to keep the pits open. But the workers' houses are still lit by oil lamps, and the only source of heating and hot water is the coal fire. The boys are thrilled by the novelty of bright light throughout the building.

They slip into seats at the back. Men sit in a row on the stage, which is normally concealed by the big screen for films.

"The big man, Mabon, isn't with us tonight," says Alun, after studying the faces of those on stage. "Business up in London, I'd say."

The scarred face of the man sitting in front of them turns round and snaps, "There's nothin' in London tha's more importan' than our concerns 'ere in the Rhondda tonight! It's 'ere 'ee should be, isn'it, the waster!"

"Yes, his clock is ticking too, Tal," agrees Dic Tic Toc.

"Good evening, comrades!" One of the leaders has stood up. The audience falls quiet.

"You all know why we are here. The Naval Company has stated that eight hundred miners will be locked out of the Ely

Colliery, Pen-y-graig next week. On Thursday, the first of September. We will all be walking out, with our tools, the evening before that. The gates will close and work will stop."

"Are you sure?" Tal, the man with the scarred face, is on his feet, and shouting across the hall. "Maybe their plan is to bring in blacklegs!"

"We'll have to stop them!" Another miner, half way down the hall, is on his feet, his fist in the air.

"Yes! Yes! No blacklegs in the valley!" The temperature is rising in the hall and several others are already on their feet. Guto notices that his brother Wil is among them, his arm punching the air right at the front.

The leader raises his hand to quieten the crowd.

"Before we come to the arrangements about how we're going to protect the pit against the company bringing in cheap labour to do our work, I'm going to ask Dai Lend Me to say a few words."

Dai is a short man with an impassive face, but he has fire in his eyes. He speaks off-the-cuff, without any notes at all.

"If we are to defeat the Naval Company, we must know more than them," says Dai in a hard voice which reaches every corner of the hall. "They have offered the worst wage rate that has ever been offered in the Rhondda. One shilling and ninepence for a ton of coal, and a penny for every ton of rock. And that offer is to the most expert and experienced workers, who are working the most difficult seams in south Wales. We cannot live on that. And neither can any miner in any other valley live on that. And no colliers will turn blackleg this time. The Fed has brought us together. The miners in other pits support the lads of the Ely pit. This is a test. If the bosses win, wages will fall throughout the Rhondda. This is not an Ely Colliery battle, it's a battle for every one of the Naval Company's pits and, let me tell you, for every pit in Wales. In unity there is strength!"

These words are followed by deafening applause. When Dai Lend Me sits back down, another man on the stage gets to his feet. The boys do not recognise him.

"I'm speaking on behalf of the Nant-gwyn Colliery miners. The Naval owns our pit too. They haven't yet threatened us with a reduction in wages, but things are difficult enough on what we get now. We held a pithead meeting at the end of a shift. We have decided to carry our tools out of Nant-gwyn next Wednesday evening. We will go on strike to support the Ely Colliery miners until the lockout is retracted."

A cheer like thunder greets this declaration. The shouting and clapping go on for several minutes. As the noise subsides, Guto sees that someone is on his feet in the front row.

"I work in the Pandy Colliery. Pandy is another of the Naval's pits. If their pits don't produce coal, the company won't make any money. I'm not going underground on Thursday. I, too, will be on strike!"

Another round of applause and calls of approval.

Tal stand up and bellows, "'Ow about all of us in the Pandy goin' on strike?"

"Yes! We'll stand together! Go for a strike!"

The Empire is in uproar.

After a few minutes, the leader stands and raises his hand.

"The Nant-gwyn Colliery miners have had an orderly meeting and have voted. That is not the case for the Pandy Colliery men. The best thing would be to clarify matters here, tonight. Is there anyone from the Pandy Colliery who opposes the proposal to go on strike?"

"No!"

"Strike!"

"There'll be no scabs in the Pandy!"

"Is there anyone unwilling to join the strike?" asks the leader.

Silence.

"There we are, then. Next Wednesday night, miners from the three pits will pick up their tools and head home. No mandrel or chisel or sledgehammer will remain in the Ely Colliery, the Nant-gwyn Colliery nor the Pandy Colliery. Over two thousand miners will be on strike!"

"Alright then, that's settled!"

"And before long, the Cambrian and Glamorgan colliers will come together to discuss striking in support of those on strike in the Naval's pits. Between them those two pits have over eight thousand men underground. It'll be a strike and a half if they come out. And we need to discuss arrangements to picket the pits against the bosses bringing in blacklegs. I declare the meeting closed."

For several minutes no one leaves the hall. There is excited chatter between the workers. The decision has given the miners new hope. They'll win this time, this is what they're telling each other. Several of the older men remember the strikes of the past, when the miners – with no wages, and with their families starving – were beaten in the end and forced back to work and into accepting the owners' rates.

But not this time, they say, slapping each other on the back.

There'll be no coal trains to the ports at Cardiff and Barry.

There'll be no money in the owners' pockets.

They'll have to agree to half a crown a day for the miners of the Ely Colliery.

At last the hard-faced, scarred-faced crowd surges out of the Empire into Dunraven Street. Some are singing. Others hurry to the Cross Keys and the White Hart to celebrate the new power in their hands. Others go on towards Llwynypia Road to the Institute, to read the paper or have a game of snooker.

Guto and Dicw stand to the left of the main door of the Empire for a little while as the crowd disperses.

"Well, we're off the starting blocks, then!" says Alun. "You can't hold miners back when they've got fire in their bellies."

"But doesn't the strike mean there'll be no money coming into the house?" asks Guto, thinking of the jug on the shelf.

"Well, we have the Fed now," explains Alun. "Every miner across south Wales pays into the South Wales Miners' Federation every week. A quarter of a million workers. Then, when an occasion like this arises and the miners strike for their rights in some of the pits, the Fed gives those miners strike pay."

"And how much will that be?" Guto asks.

"Well, five shillings a week for boys and ten shillings a week for men."

"Will the miners who've been injured or who can't work get money too?" Dicw asks.

"Oh, the Fed will help their families too, you can be sure of it," Alun assures him. "Well, lads, time for me to go on night shift. Hey, I won't have to say or do that much longer!"

"No, you won't," Dic says. "The clock is ticking."

Guto and Dicw go back up the main street before turning past Ebenezer for Eleanor Street. As they had passed Bertorelli's, they had seen that the place was chock-a-block. Many who were at the meeting had headed straight for the Italians' comfortable seating. Pietro was outside, winding the blind back into its casing for the night.

"*Ciao*, big men!" he'd said, with a wide smile as he recognised the two friends. "Fancy some pop after the meeting? Aren't you thirsty?"

"No, we're going home now," Guto had answered.

"See you again, *buona sera*! Good evening!"

Before this they had passed Elias Davies' shop. Although the shop was closed, they had seen the proprietor outside the door, dressed in a black overcoat with a fur collar. He was wearing a silk top hat and holding a cigar between the fingers of his right hand. Beside him stood a clerk in a bowler hat and dark suit, clutching a hard-backed notebook and a pencil.

"Over there!" the clerk had said in English to his master. Pointing at one of the miners who was walking past in the flat-capped crowd, he had added, "Over there, that's one of them."

"What's his name?" Elias Davies had asked.

"Ken Thomas. His wife has bought a hat on the never-never ..."

"Ken Thomas!" the shop owner had yelled. "Come here." Then he had added in Welsh, "Come over here. My clerk tells me that your wife is in debt to the shop. She's had a hat ..."

"Yes, yes," the man called Ken Thomas had answered. "She's paying threepence a week every Saturday ..."

"The whole payment on Saturday or return the hat," Elias Davies had said.

"But it's on the never-never ... we can't afford ... and anyway, food has to come first ..."

"Things have changed now. When you're on strike she'll default on the payments. Pay the whole lot on Saturday or bring the hat back. Put it in the book," he had said to his clerk.

"But ..."

"Go home!"

"That one over there is Stanley Phillips," says the clerk.

"Hey, Stanley Phillips ..." and Elias Davies had made the same threat to him about a coat his wife had purchased on account from his shop.

"What's the never-never?" Dicw had asked.

"You get something from the shop and you don't pay for it," Guto had explained. "Say a hat costs five shillings. Maybe you'd pay sixpence down and then pay threepence a week for twenty-five weeks. You end up paying more than the price, but you don't have to have saved up the money first. You get what you want but pay for it a bit at a time over a number of weeks."

"Do many people do that, then?"

"That's what every couple that marry do these days. They furnish the house and buy everything and spend years paying for it."

"Most of the wages goes to paying the shops back, is it?"

"Yes, yes, that's how it is. And then when the first baby arrives, more things are needed on the never-never. And when the children grow, they want things on the never-never."

"Why is it called the 'never-never', then?"

"Oh, there's somewhere in Australia called Never-Never, according to Alun. He should know – he has a brother out in Australia. It's some remote place, far from anywhere. It takes you forever to get back. Being in debt on the never-never is the same idea. You never return from being poor."

"It's alright if wages rise, I suppose," Dicw had said.

"But hard if they fall."

"And Elias Davis is worried that he won't get paid by the miners' wives during the strike?"

Guto had hesitated before replying, and then said, "I wouldn't be surprised if most of the men don't know that their wives have debts. Nor their daughters either."

Dicw is quiet for the rest of the way home.

Guto looks at the door of his family's home before stepping inside. The door has been painted black and it shines like newly-cut coal. Every other door in Eleanor Street is a darkish brown, but Alun had come home one day with a tin of black paint from the timbermen's workshop at the pithead. It was paint for the works trams, and he set to one

Saturday afternoon to paint the door.

"There we are!" he'd said when he'd finished. "It's the same colour as everything else in the valley now!"

Inside Number 17 Eleanor Street, Guto tells his mother what happened at the meeting.

"So the Glamorgan'll be on strike too, will it?" she asks. "Wiliam hasn't been on strike before and he doesn't remember the lockout of 1898. But his father does. Six months with no wages. We spent every penny we had to keep us alive. Families were turned out of their homes because they couldn't pay their rent to the owners. And it was back to the pit in the end without having gained a thing."

"Who do we pay our rent to, Mam?"

"The Naval built these houses – a whole terrace for the miners ..."

"So the pit owners own the houses of the miners who are on strike!"

"No. Not all of them. They sold some of the houses to raise money to open more mines in the Rhondda."

"Who bought the houses, then? Not the colliers, I'll bet."

"Shopkeepers, businesspeople in the main street, one or two colliery managers ..."

"And who owns our house?"

"We pay rent to Wilkins the grocer."

Wiliam comes into the house just then. His face is flushed, as if he has sprinted home. Beti notices he has a gash on his forehead, across his left eyebrow.

"I didn't notice that cut above your eye when you were having your bath," his mother says to him.

"It was there," Wiliam says emphatically. "It was probably hidden by coal dust. I walked into a rock where the roof was low."

Chapter 6

"So every mandrel and crowbar has been taken out of the Naval pit," says Alun. "If the bosses try to play dirty, there'll be no tools available to any idiot blacklegs."

Alun the Ox, Dic Tic Toc, Guto and Dicw are sitting round the small table in the window of Bertorelli's cafe.

"Try to play dirty?" Dic says. "That's exactly what they're going to do, as sure as today's a Thursday."

"What's a blackleg, then?" asks Dicw.

"The bosses will try to break the strike, you see," Alun says. "They have to continue getting coal out of the ground one way or another or they'll have no profit. They'll be scouring the Valleys for miners who'll come and work the pits that are on strike."

"Will they find anyone like that?"

"All the miners are in full employment," says Alun. "There's such a demand for Welsh coal that there's a shortage of men to work underground. But more arrive every day – from England, from the Welsh countryside, and even from overseas. We've still got men coming here from the slate-quarrying areas up north – it's only seven years since their three-year lockout, and their industry hasn't really recovered yet. All of these men and their families have seen great poverty. They'll do anything for money."

"And what happens then?"

"The miners that are on strike will try to stop any and every blackleg from working in our pits, of course."

"And we'll have to be ready for that in the morning," says Dic Tic Toc, looking at his pocket watch.

"But why have these workers got only one leg that's black?" says Guto. "In our house, when you come home from the pit you've got black*legs* – you're black all over."

"Ha! That's a good one!" Alun says. He looks over his shoulder to take a look at the rest of the cafe. The tables are set very close together, with four chairs each, but most tables have only one person sitting at them. Nevertheless, the chatter in the cafe runs from table to table, even though the customers are seated at different ones.

"Hey, Cabbage White!"

A stocky man on the furthest table – whose real name is Gwyn – raises his shoulders.

"How's your potatoes this year?"

"The early ones were so small they were like marbles," answers the man, "but, to be honest, they're cropping pretty well now. I'm getting half a bucket from every plant."

"It's the manure from the pit ponies what's made the difference," shouts another man across the room.

"Yes, we've seen you, Gwyn," says another, "taking potato and cabbage leaves in a sack for the ponies and then fetching a sackful of the smelly stuff back for that veg patch of yours."

"Better than stinking out in the mine," Gwyn replies.

"Oh, the rats down there would eat it all up in no time, don't you worry," says another man, adding his twopenn'oth. "They eat anything and everything. When I started in the pit as a lad, Dad always told me to eat my lunch before starting my shift – in case the rats attacked me for it!"

"Cabbage White is a very keen gardener in the People's Allotments up on the side of the mountain," Alun explains to the lads. He raises his head to continue the conversation across the cafe. "No disease on the potatoes this year, then?"

"No, the crop's been very clean."

"No rotting of the stems?"

"No, not a single blackleg this year."

"Thanks, Gwyn. This here lad wanted to know what a blackleg is."

"Well, he knows now. It's a disease!" shouted Gwyn.

"True enough!"

"What's needed is to keep them out!" Men on every table in the cafe add their voices to the conversation now.

"Once the stem of one plant in the row is infected, the whole lot go black," explains Gwyn. "The danger is that it spreads along the row, then on to the next ... You can lose a whole year's crop."

"Exactly like the mine," says a voice from the corner. "If one or two blacklegs are seen to be getting paid, it weakens things for everyone. There's a danger of the strike collapsing."

"We've got a hard time ahead of us," says Dic Tic Toc, looking at the clock on the wall behind the counter.

Just then, Pietro arrives with the order for the whole table.

"*Buona sera* boys! Tea for you, Alun, am I right?"

"Yes, a little pot of strong tea."

"And a little jug of hot water later on, is it, Alun?"

"Yes, my usual, Pietro," Alun confirms.

"Oh, he's a smart one, is Alun," says Pietro. "He asks for strong tea and then he sits here all evening and calls for another jug of hot water. He gets the water for free, of course, and drinks the same tea all night!"

"He's a Cardi, what do you expect?" says Dic Tic Toc.

"It's pretty weak by nine o'clock, I'll have you know!" laughs Alun

"And milk for you, Dic."

"Thank you very much."

"And Mountain Pop for these big men."

"Mountain Pop?" queries Dicw.

"From Welsh Hills in Porth!" says Pietro with a broad smile. "*Una* cherryade, *una* burdock. Enjoy them, boys."

The cafe proprietor moves smoothly between tables, collecting the odd empty cup, and with a word for everyone he passes. It's lovely in the cafe, thinks Guto. Lots of chat, lots of laughs. There's room to sit and it's warm and cosy without the fug of drying clothes that clings to every kitchen in every house.

He looks about. He sees that most of the men here are lodgers. Single men, not men with families. Men who are grateful to have somewhere to go to socialise without having to dig deep into their pockets all night. He knew the Italians never rushed anyone nor moved them off their tables. As with Alun, every one of them was welcome to stay with their one cup of tea or coffee all evening if they felt like it.

When Guto and Dicw rise from the table to go home for supper, Pietro is at the counter.

"Big men! Come with me to see the back of the cafe!" He waves his left arm enthusiastically, opening the little hatch on the counter to let himself out. Then he pushes open the door at the back and the boys see a woman with dark, wavy hair mixing something in a bowl. She smiles at them, flashing very white teeth. Behind her there is a girl with a dark complexion with her hands submerged in washing up water in a huge sink. She studies the boys carefully with her dark eyes.

"This is Emilia, my wife. She is mixing *salsicce* ... how do you say? *Salsicce*?

"Sausages?" suggests Dicw.

"Yes, *bene. Salsicce* ... sausage. Sausage rolls. They sell well in the cafe. Emilia, *posso presentarle Guto e Dicw*." Pietro introduces the two lads to his wife.

"*Piacere*," Emilia says. "*Come sta*?"

"Emilia has not learned much Welsh yet," explains Pietro. "She works here in the back. She's asking, '*Come sta*?' – 'How are you?' And you say, '*Bene, grazie*' – Well, thank you!"

"*Bene, grazie. Bene, grazie*," say Guto and Dicw.

"And this is Nina," Pietro introduces the girl at the sink. "Nina, *cara*, our daughter. She has been living with *Nonno e Nonna* back in Bardi for several years – her grandfather and grandmother, isn't it? She goes to the St Gabriel and St Raphael School now and she starts to learn English. Maybe you know? She'll be learning Welsh in the cafe, of course!"

The lads knew about the Catholic school on Primrose Street, behind Eleanor Street. That was the school the children of all the Irish and Italian and Spanish people of Cwm Rhondda attended. There was a church next to the school and Guto had heard chanting in a very strange language when there had been a service in progress with the doors open, as he had passed on a fine summer's day. He recalls seeing a baptismal party there too. There had been a big crowd outside, every family in their best clothes and looking splendid. On that occasion there had been much laughter and jollity.

Nina turns to face the boys. Once again the dark eyes survey them carefully, without a hint of a smile on her lips. She must be about the same age as them, thinks Guto.

"Hello, Nina," he says to her.

Nina turns back to the pots and pans she had been washing and throws herself into the task with such zeal that the dishwater sloshes about in foamy waves.

"I have one son too," explains Pietro. "But Aldo has gone back to Bardi over the winter. He is one year older than Nina. He is back on the farm in Val Ceno in Bardi – with *Nonno e Nonna*. They are old now. Aldo is there over the winter. Cutting firewood. It's cold in the mountains of Bardi. Winter is hard. So we will not see Aldo until Easter."

Guto recalls that, during the summer, he'd noticed the young Italian. He was a tall youth with dark, curly hair and was always dressed in clean white trousers. He pushed a wooden cart up and down the Tonypandy terraces shouting "*Gelato! Hufen iâ!* Ice cream!" all summer. The cart was painted yellow and red, with the name *Bertorelli's Ice Cream* on it in fancy lettering. When Guto had a halfpenny to spare, there was nothing better than a *gelato* from the Bertorelli's cart.

"Aldo Gelato?" Guto says, which pleases the father.

"Ah! You know him! Everyone in Tonypandy and Llwynypia knows Aldo. Aldo is a good boy. Do you like *gelato*? Eh? Silly question – everyone likes Bertorelli's *gelato*! Hey, big men – come over here."

Pietro opens a large metal cupboard with pipes and gas cylinders beside it. The lads can see all kinds of tins inside the cupboard, each veiled by a thin layer of ice. This must be an ice chamber, thinks Guto. He has heard of them, but has never seen one. They were the contraptions in which the Italians of the valley made and stored their ice cream.

In no time at all, Pietro has lifted a particular tin out of the cupboard and opened its lid.

"*Gelato Vanilia Bertorelli!*" he announces. "The best *gelato* in Cwm Rhondda. No! The best *gelato* in Wales! Ha! Where are the wafers ...?"

Shortly afterwards they are leaving the cafe, each licking a square of ice cream clamped between two wafers.

"These Italians are friendly, aren't they?" Dicw says.

"They are warm and full of life," agrees Guto. "And they must like sharing."

"We hardly know them, but Mister Bertorelli treated us like kings."

"Maybe he's missing Aldo," says Guto after a while.

They take their time climbing Ebenezer Road to reach Eleanor Street, which runs behind the main street. They see that the street is empty; there are no children playing outside. As they approach Dicw's house, Guto sees that Moc, his father, is standing in his best clothes outside the front door.

There are another half dozen or so men there in dark clothes. The others are all miners from the Pandy Colliery, thinks Guto.

As they go up the steps from the street towards the door, Moc steps forward and places his hand on Dicw's shoulder.

"I'm very sorry, Dicw. I'm afraid Watcyn has lost the battle."

Guto notices that every man is holding his cap in his hands.

He turns to say something to his friend, but Dicw has run indoors to the rest of his family.

On this day, the blackest door in the street is this one, thinks Guto.

Chapter 7

When Guto reaches his own home, there are no pit clothes drying on the guard in front of the fire. As there will be no need for work clothes the following day nor, perhaps, for several more days, Beti has taken them all out to the back. She will have one backbreaking day of washing them all and then a break from the wooden washtub, the dolly and the washboard.

But the strike is causing her more work in another arena.

"I'll need you tomorrow, Guto," she tells her son. "The Co-op has promised us bread and tins of vegetables and meat to make *cawl* for the strikers' children. We don't have to pay until money starts coming in again and, unlike the never-never, the Co-op won't charge us interest. It's the workers that own the Co-op, you see."

"And who's the 'we', Mam?"

"Well, the children's welfare committee, of course! We're being allowed to use the big vestry in Ebenezer chapel on the main street. We can boil up the *cawl* there and have the children in together every day to eat. That's what happens with every strike. The first to suffer every time are the children."

"How old are the children?" asks Eira from her seat in the corner.

"The under tens."

"And where will we have our food, then?" asks the girl.

"Food will be on the table here, as usual."

"Will you be going down to the vestry to help, Eira?" Guto asks.

"I'll be at work all day! It's completely impossible for me to go."

"I had been hoping to go down to make sure there were no blacklegs trying to get to Pandy pit tomorrow morning," Guto says.

"That's men's work, *crwt*," chides his mother. "There'll be plenty to keep you busy in the vestry."

"Llew, will you be getting hot *cawl* tomorrow, then?" Guto asks his brother. Llew has improved a little since his last bad patch, and is squatting in the corner beside the fire. He's had another little bout of coughing but his eyes are less drowsy.

Dewi has got hold of two sticks from the store of kindling and is poking Llew in the stomach and upper arm.

"Hey, Dewi! Stop that nonsense," his mother says. "What do you think you are – a policeman?"

Eira goes to sit next to Llew and, while the rest of the family talk about the strike, pulls him to her and quietly rubs the pain away from his belly.

"Will there be policemen in the valley tomorrow, then, Mam?" Guto asks.

"If there's any danger of the colliery bosses losing something, you can be sure that the Glamorgan Constabulary will be here in a line to protect their interests."

"There were hundreds of policemen and even the army in Cwm Cynon a few years ago, weren't there?" Guto says. "Just think – policemen and soldiers attacking ordinary workers!"

"Oh, it won't come to that in Tonypandy, don't you worry."

"Come here, Dewi." Guto grabs the toddler and places him on his lap as he sits down at the table. He reaches for a piece of newspaper and a pencil and starts doodling in the margin of the page.

"You saw Alun bringing his work tools home from the Pandy pit today, didn't you? Well, here's what they are, Dewi. This is a mandrel, you see. The miner cuts the coal out of the seam with this and the timberman has to make a hole to put the post in to support the roof of the tunnel. You see the points both ends of the head? This bit's iron, you see, Dewi – and it's with this the miner cuts the big pieces of coal, but he needs to hit the coal really hard. And where he's working is a very small space, and the roof is low. That's why there's a short handle on the madrel and spade, so they can be used in awkward places."

Guto draws a picture of a mandrel and a spade on the edge of the page.

"Sometimes the coal's even too awkward for a mandrel, and black powder has to be used to blow it loose. For that the collier needs a steel drill. He makes a deep hole in the coal to put the black powder in.

"Then one of the butties – the young boys – lifts the big pieces of coal into the tram that runs on wheels along the level. At the end the tram is pulled by the little pit ponies to the bottom of the shaft and then it goes up to the surface. Off it goes then on the train to the docks in Cardiff and Barry and across the sea to lands far away. This is a picture of a tram, Dewi, this is."

"And this is Alun's spade to scoop up the smaller pieces of coal and the really little pieces that fall out of the tram and then Alun makes a place to position the wooden pit props to keep the roof up. The mandrel and the spade have wooden handles and they sometimes break. So they have to have spare handles for spades and mandrels, and for the big hammers as well – the 'sledge'. You've heard Mam say to Dad that he's as 'stupid as a sledge', haven't you? Well, on top of the wooden handle, the head of the sledge is a big hard lump of iron – like a giant hammer. If all else fails, Dad fetches the sledge and gives the rock or the coal a massive whack. So here's a picture of a sledge ...

"These are the tools of the miner's trade, Dewi. They keep them in work. But there's a strike now, and this gear is all here, at home."

The door opens and Moc comes in.

"How are the Mainwarings, Moc?" Beti asks.

"Despairing, as you can imagine."

"Was Emrys there?"

"Yes. A father burying his son – again. That's how it is in this valley."

"Didn't our Wil come home with you?"

"Committee meeting in the Institute – the Fed officials at the Glamorgan."

"Is the Glamorgan on strike, then?"

"Not yet. But they'll have to give the colliers from the Pandy, Nant-gwyn and the Ely a hand in due course."

* * *

Not many of the Naval collieries' hooters sounded the next morning. The usual Glamorgan and the Cambrian wails were heard, but they were not followed by the klaxons of the Ely, the Pandy nor Nant-gwyn.

Moc and Wil had got up to go to work in the Llwynypia mine as usual. Alun was up early as well, as he is now sleeping in the chair by the fire. Being on strike, he doesn't need to work at night. There hasn't been much sleep in the other terraced houses in the valley either. The striking miners got up at the usual time. It was difficult for them not to, as their body clocks are so used to the pit timetable. Work to support the strike got Guto out of bed early that morning in Number 17.

"I said that going to the Co-op was your work this morning, *crwt*," his mother told him.

"The Co-op doesn't open for another two hours, Mam. And I'm not a *crwt* any more – I'm fourteen!"

"Let him come with us, Beti," Alun says. "He needs to see a bit of the collier's life before starting in the pit in the new year."

"Do we need to take a mandrel handle with us, in case of trouble?" Guto asks.

"No we don't, you blockhead!" Alun says. "You'll attract trouble if you're caught carrying a weapon. Keep your hands clean, that's what's important today. Keep your eye on what's happening – there are enough of us."

"Would you like me to carry the hot water out to the washtub for you before going, Mam?" Guto asks.

"No thank you very much!" she replies curtly. "I did that before you were up."

Heavy hobnailed boots drumming the cobbles is music to Guto's ears. This morning he's not hearing it from his bedroom, above the sound of his brother and sister breathing. He's out in the sharp morning air, walking in step with the colliers. He has a cap on his head, a muffler round his neck and a broad smile on his face. He walks like a soldier but there is only the sound of boots today – none of the miners is carrying a tin jack for water or a tommy-box for food.

The gates to the Pandy Colliery pithead are reached too soon for his liking. That morning he would have enjoyed another mile or two of walking with the procession. He is amazed to see hundreds there already. The tall gates have been chained and locked from the inside. There is no one to be seen at the pithead works but the lights of the office are on.

"We can' see them," says Tal, the miner with the scarred face. "But you can bet your boots tha' they can see us."

"There's no sign of anyone going to work today," says another collier. "The wagons and engines aren't moving. No one can go in or out except through this here gate and we're too strong for anyone to try."

By first light, the crowd of miners extends a long way back from the pit. There is no sound from the pithead wheel of chains or gear turning. It is plain that the cage is taking no one down to cut coal.

With this realisation, the miners begin to relax and chat. There is banter and leg pulling, and occasional laughter.

Suddenly the sound of hobnailed boots running from the direction of Pen-y-graig reaches them.

"Police!" shouts the first of two messengers who have been sent from the Ely Colliery. "A special train has reached the pithead and there are dozens of policemen pouring out of it."

"From Cardiff and Swansea, we reckon," says the second messenger, once he's caught his breath.

Guto feels a surge of excitement go down his backbone. What does this mean? The mine owners were up to something, that much was certain.

"Have the gates been opened?"

"No, they've not come near the gates yet."

"Are there blacklegs on the train?"

"No one's seen any. But there may be another train on the way."

"There's enough looking for work in the docks at the other end of this line, in Barry – we wouldn't be surprised if the bosses tried to attract some of them here as cheap labour."

"And to spoil the craft of mining at the same time!"

"They understand neither rock nor coal."

The mood of the miners is intensifying. Guto can feel the crowd's agitation around him. The next minute, a man has climbed onto a low wall near the gates of the mine. He recognises him – Dai Lend Me, one of the leaders from the stage at the Empire.

"I'm going to ask half of you to go to the Ely pit. The fact that the police have arrived is cause for concern. They – the owners – have had more time to plan their tactics for the Ely Colliery as it is they who have sacked the colliers and closed the works. They may have a trick up their sleeves. Right. Surface workers from Pandy pit and miners from Levels 2, 3 and 4, stay here. Everyone else – come with me to see what skulduggery is going on at the Ely."

Guto knows that Alun is a timberman on Level 6. He sticks close to him as the miners separate into two groups.

"Hey, *crwt*, where d'you think you're going?" asks one of the strikers. "You don't work with us yet!"

"Dai Lend Me didn't say anything about that," Guto shoots back. "He named the workers to stay here – and I wasn't among those."

"Let him come along," Alun says. "It'll be easier to keep an eye on him if he's with us."

Once Dai has got the two groups organised, he goes on to prime them.

"I'm coming with you to Pen-y-graig. If there's any trouble with police truncheons, we'll have to get the Ely lads to lend us mandrel handles. The rest of you, you stay here in front of the Pandy gates. Stand close together and don't let anyone go through the gates to work. Emrys and Ken, if anything happens here, run over to us to let us know. Right then, the rest of you, off we go to Pen-y-graig."

Guto feels the hairs on the back of his neck stand up like a hedgehog's spines as he marches with the miners. And they were marching now, not walking in a procession. The nails of their boots pounding the streets echoes across the town in unison. A group of miners had suddenly turned into an army, ready to fight for their rights.

Up Tylacelyn Road and then a fork to the right to go along Pen-y-graig Road. The men then cut up a narrow path behind two chapels. Above them they can see the steep embankment of the Great Western railway line, which runs to the mines at Ely, Nant-gwyn and Cwm Clydach.

"There are two railways in this part of Cwm Rhondda," Alun explains to Guto. "The Great Western that runs to the mines on this side and then down to the docks at Barry, and the Taff Vale that runs down the valley to the Glamorgan pit in Llwynypia and the Pandy and takes the coal down to Pontypridd and Cardiff docks. That's how the owners can divide and rule with the railway workers – playing one against the other and keeping wages low. Today it looks as if they've brought the policemen on the Great Western."

They hear a shout from the top of the embankment.

"Up here! We're in the old quarry the other side of the sidings!"

The Pandy miners – with Guto in their midst – climb up the steep embankment to the metal fence between them and the railway. Guto notices that some of the older miners' breathing is laboured by the time they reach the top. The pernicious dust, he thinks. Years of working underground in confined spaces without enough fresh air has filled up their lungs with coal dust. Hard scars, like heavy rocks, have formed in their lungs and not much oxygen now reaches their blood. One or two of the faces are turning blue.

In front of them, Guto sees the headframe of the main winding wheel above the shaft that normally lets cages of miners down to lower levels. Behind it is a smaller wheel for the second shaft – the ventilation shaft. There are large, imposing buildings around the base of the headframes – the drumhouse for the winch cable, a tall brick chimney, offices, workshops, stores and piles of timber. Beyond the main Great Western line right in front of them the surface of the works is covered with other lines, with scores of wagons, some full of coal and some waiting to be filled. One or two of these tracks disappear into the buildings at the pithead.

"Blacklegs!" rings out the cry from the old quarry on the other side of the railway.

Chapter 8

The two messengers climb over the wire fence and run across the line in the direction of the shout.

"Over the fence, boys," Dai Lend Me calls out, "but stay on the line so we can hear what's happening and where we're supposed to go."

In no time at all one of the messengers comes back.

"Dai! The policemen have gone into the powerhouse and the other buildings on the surface. They're afraid we'll attack the gear and smash it up."

"Destroy our own workplace? They've got the wrong end of the stick if they think that. We want to go back to work, not smash the works!"

"It's the powerhouse that supplies electricity to the whole pit. They're keeping an eye on that," says one of the Ely miners. "That's what lets the cage down and lifts it back up and pumps water out of the bottom of the mine. The mine will flood and we'll be out here for ever and never get back to work if the power goes ..."

"Yes, yes," says Dai impatiently. "We know all that. Now where are these blacklegs?"

"They'll be coming down the main way from Pen-y-graig. Some have been seen coming along the railway line from Williamstown. They're standing by at the moment, waiting to see what'll happen."

"And what do you want us to do?"

"We'll have to come out of the quarry over there now to stand across the line. You lot come towards us from this side and then we'll block all the lines between the Ely Colliery and Pontypridd. No train will be able to carry coal from this pit to the docks, and no blacklegs will be able to get into the works this way, through the back door."

"Right," Dai says, "did you hear all that? Across the line towards the Ely colliers it is. Keep calm. We don't want to see you falling and injuring yourselves. Although, with some of you being so headstrong, the lines might come off worse than your skulls."

The miners are in good spirits. The sun is rising higher with each passing minute and every hollow and fold of the valley is revealed. The first of September, Guto thinks. The season is turning. There was a nip in the air in the early mornings and the hawthorn and rowan berries blazed red on the slopes of Mynydd Brithweunydd and Mynydd Pen-y-graig, flanking this part of the valley. In this dawn light, the shadows were long and behind them he could see the big metal frame of the pithead wheel, like a threatening black eagle.

"The police! There they are!"

A shout goes up from the Ely miners. By now the Pandy miners have joined them on the railway line and, standing in a wall ten deep, there are enough of them to close it.

Guto turns to look behind him once more. He sees dark ranks of police officers emerging from the pithead storerooms, forming a tight wall of heavy coats, their helmets sitting low on their foreheads. The ranks of policemen start to walk slowly and deliberately towards the crowd of strikers.

"Go to the back!" Alun shouts to Guto. "We weren't expecting this! They could charge us with truncheons! If they do, run for your life – up Mynydd Pen-y-graig. You're quicker than those stocky men over there. You can get ahead and then work your way back towards Tonypandy and come down and go home. Now, get to the back!"

Guto obeys immediately. The scene is terrifying. A wall of tall, broad policemen approaching threateningly. On the command of one of their officers, each pulls a truncheon from his belt and Guto sees them glinting in the morning sun. He has seen truncheons hanging from the belts of policemen on duty on the main street in Tonypandy on a Saturday night, of course. Two foot of solid wood encased in hard black leather. But he has never before seen such truncheons out of their cases. He is relieved to be able to slip to the back and work his way towards the side of the mountain, away from the railway lines.

He looks down the railway and sees maybe a dozen men hiding behind a signal box about a hundred yards down the valley. It's clear these are the men attempting to go into the mine to do a day's work and earn a day's pay. But they don't look as if they'll get any closer.

"They've stopped!" The message travels through the crowd of miners and reaches Guto's ears. He climbs onto the wheel of a wagon standing in a siding nearby to see what is happening between the ranks of policemen and miners. It's clear that the police are not planning on getting any closer to the miners – but their truncheons are still in their hands.

Then Guto sees a man in an expensive-looking coat and bowler hat make his way through the ranks of police. He has a briefcase in his hand. The chief police officer comes from behind to stand at his side.

"Who speaks for you?" the policeman shouts to the miners. A murmur spreads through the crowd and three of the Ely colliers step smartly forward.

"We three. But we won't give our names."

Very wise, thinks Guto. It was always the way in the Valleys that those who spoke for the workers then lost their jobs in the pit. The owners had a list of names of men considered 'troublesome' and it was difficult for such men to get work in scores of mines once their name was on the list.

"Tha's Mister Llewelyn 'oo's with the copper, isn'it?" asks an old miner next to Guto.

"I think you're right," says his partner, squinting to focus. "Yes, it's Mister Llewelyn. The top dog, I'll be damned! Look at his moustache there, twirled up at the ends like a bull's horns!"

Leonard Llewelyn, general manager of all David Thomas' pits, manages over ten thousand miners in the mines in mid-Cwm Rhondda. These pits produce half of the Rhondda's coal.

"Take one of the Pandy boys with you," comes a shout from the midst of the Ely miners.

"Lend me a fag." Every one of the workers hears the harsh voice of Dai Lend Me asking for a cigarette and then for someone to lend him a match with which to light it. Dragging on his smoke, he joins the three from Pen-y-graig. A knowing and sardonic laugh spreads amongst the miners. If the authorities knew their men, it won't be hard to work out that Dai Lend Me is one of the four who are now walking towards the officials. Leonard Llewelyn and the chief police offer come forward to meet them.

The crowd has stilled, but it isn't possible to hear the conversation. From his position on the wagon, Guto can see the two officials standing straight-backed and important, full of the authority their positions bestow. They are several inches taller than the four miners and are dressed formally. The miners stand straight-backed too, their shoulders much more muscular than the two authority figures, and their large, scarred hands moving eloquently in the air as they speak.

At long last, the two authority figures nod. And then the four miners nod. There is no handshake, but it is clear some understanding has been reached. The four miners return to their colleagues. One of the Ely contingent speaks on their behalf.

"Right, we may not see eye to eye, but at least we've come to some sort of understanding. The first thing is that they don't want us to attack the pit or the buildings or the gear and create a ruckus. We told them that wasn't the intention. We told him not one of us is carrying a weapon."

"True enough! But they're waving truncheons at us, for goodness' sake!"

"Yes, they've promised to put away the rolling pins!" says the speaker. And just as he says this, Guto can see the policemen reattaching their truncheons to their belts and walking back to the pithead buildings.

"We've said that we don't want blacklegs to come in to do our work. They've said there's no opportunity for anyone to work here. A lockout is a lockout, they say."

"What about the scoundrels down the line, hiding beside the signal box, then?" shouts another harsh voice.

"They say they hadn't seen them. Just some opportunists who think they can make a few pennies to fill their stomachs."

"We all know how that feels!" shouts another collier. "That's why we're striving for a fair wage."

"There'll be no wagons going down the line from the Ely today, or during the lockout, they say. But this line goes to the Cambrian in Cwm Clydach as well. The police say that coal from Cwm Clydach can go to the docks."

"But Leonard Llewelyn runs the Cambrian in Cwm Clydach and the Naval. If he and David Thomas are still getting money out of the valley, he's not going to miss the money lost from the Naval pits, is he?"

"That's true," says the main speaker. "But the Cambrian boys aren't on strike yet. We can't stop their coal or we'll be hindering our fellow workers. No, we're agreed on this – no trains from the Ely but the line is open to Cwm Clydach."

"Some of us had better stay here to keep an eye on things, that's what I say!"

Most strongly agree, and they organise two-hour shifts between them for the rest of the day and through the night too. Everything seems to be coming to a close and the Pandy miners are on the verge of going back to see how things are at their own pit when one miner shouts, "How about we teach those fellas sneaking about by the signals a lesson?"

"What do you mean?"

"We could move to the side. Half this side of the line, Pandy lads the other side, as though we've decided to leave them and we miners are going back to the pit ..."

"Yeah!" The eyes of another one of the men sparkles as the plan sinks in. "And then close the circle?"

"Get a good look at their faces – and let them know how we usually deal with blacklegs!"

"But no one's to lay a finger on them, mind!" warns the main speaker as he gives his approval.

The whole thing works as if they had been rehearsing the move for weeks. The miners that were in the middle of the line disperse outwards, moving away from each side of the line. Some turn away from the signal box, as if they have completely lost interest in the men there. Some of the miners raise their arms, as if they are bidding each other farewell.

Gradually, like nervous mice, eleven men slowly emerge. Some of them start to walk cautiously up the line. Before long, the rest join them.

By now, several of the Pandy miners have climbed over the wire fence, some going down the embankment out of sight of the blacklegs – but then they very skilfully walk quietly along the bottom of the embankment in the direction of Williamstown. Before long they are further down the line than the eleven.

They, meanwhile, are growing bolder and walk on confidently, believing that they'll reach the pit offices to offer themselves to do whatever work needs doing. They do not see a line of Pandy miners climbing back up the embankment behind them, then climbing across the fence and walking quietly until there is no escape.

As one, the rest of the Pandy boys climb back over the fence to form a line in front of the eleven. The Ely miners join them on the other side and in seconds the pincer movement round the would-be blacklegs is complete.

The eleven stand like cornered rabbits. The ring of miners doesn't close in on them, as they fear. No miner raises his voice, they just stare at the eleven with pure contempt.

Eventually, Dai Lend Me breaks the silence. He takes three steps towards them.

"And you're planning on being blacklegs, are you? Maybe you're not familiar with the way we do things in the Valleys and you don't respect the miners' rules, so here they are for you. If you are ever caught trying any underhand tricks while we're fighting for our rights, your windows and doors will be covered in black tar. Your names will be dirt in the valley. Shops won't dare serve you. I see one of you has a track record in this sort of thing."

He raises his hand and points at the face of one of the would-be blacklegs, a man with a high forehead and a thin face.

"Who else would I expect to see among the first blacklegs but George the Traitor. I remember you. You were always a selfish devil. And now I've got all of your faces committed to memory, every one. Now, turn round and go home – and don't ever do this to us again!"

A gap opens up in the circle to let the eleven walk down towards Williamstown. With that, except for those on duty for the first picket shift, the miners disperse.

Chapter 9

"*Buon giorno*, Guto! Good morning!"

Later that morning, as he crosses Tonypandy's main street in front of a tramcar on its way down from Pen-y-graig, Guto spots Pietro cleaning the windows of Bertorelli's. Guto is on his way from the Co-op with a huge box full of tins and bread.

"Planning a big dinner, Guto?" the Italian remarks.

"For the children," Guto explains. "The strikers' children. They're coming down to Ebenezer chapel for dinner today."

"Ah!" Pietro says, immediately grasping the situation. "No money and no food in the valley. It was like that in Val Ceno."

"Were you on strike in Italy too?"

"No, no. But we were poor. No money on the farm of *Nonno e Nonna*. Lots of children. *Molti bambinos*. Always the empty stomach. Money from the hen's eggs, money from the goat's cheeses – all going to pay the rent. *Il suo terrible!* The rent going to a fat man living in a big house in Bologna!"

"And no coal mines either?"

"No, no work. So Papà – Amadeo Bertorelli – walked from the farm in the mountains. Down to the rich, flat land. Asked and asked – but no, no work. Walked to Milano. Worked a little. Walked to France. Worked picking fruit and grapes. Reached London. But people were nasty in the big city. Then the Rhondda. Ah! A big welcome and open a cafe!"

"There's another Italian cafe in Tonypandy. Is that what they did too?"

"*Sì, sì.* Yes, indeed. The Carinis in *plazza* Pandy, the Melardis in *strada* de Winton and the Servinis in the same *strada*. And there are others in Llwynypia and Treherbert and down in Porth and Pontypridd. And you know what, Guto – we all come from Val Ceno and the town of Bardi. Everyone knows each other!"

"What sort of a town is Bardi? Aren't you homesick for it?"

"Oh, I have a pain in my heart all the time. Bardi is a beautiful town, with a castle on a rock, something like Tonypandy in the number of people. But very old. Not a new town with electricity and tramcars like Tonypandy. Things are very slow in Bardi – and there is no work there. So we are Rhondda Italians now – one hundred per cent Italians, but also one hundred per cent Welsh."

"Will you go back to your old home in Bardi?"

"Ah! Papà went back – *Nonno e Nonna* were very lonely. He went back to his mother and father, but then he came back here with Mama! And me – I did go back, and came back to Tonypandy and brought Emilia with me. And now, Aldo is back there ... Ah! Who knows?"

"Bardi ..." Guto says to himself. He likes the sound of the name. "Bardi sounds like 'Berdare or 'Berdulais here in Wales, doesn't it?"

"Ah, Guto! *La verità!* The truth, you have it! Speaking Welsh is like speaking Italian. We open our mouths properly to speak – like we open our mouths wide to sing. We say every letter clearly, like the Welsh – the 'o' is a big 'O', the 'a' is a big 'A'. The words fill the mouth. You like to talk? Of course! And me too. But there is a story about the name Bardi. Two minutes, and then you can go to the chapel with that heavy box. Have you heard of Hannibal? He and his army attacked Rome a long, long time ago. You remember the story? And he crossed the Alps. You remember? With what?"

"Elephants!"

"Yes, very good. It's the truth. An army of elephants crossing the Alps. But one elephant died before it could reach Rome. And you know what his name was? Bardus. And you know where they buried him? Beside the river at Val Ceno – and that's how Bardi got its name! But there is no food in Bardi today. Everyone is poor. Hey, you know what, Guto, if an elephant died in Bardi today, they'd eat it, not bury it! What's in the box, Guto?"

"Mam and the other mothers are making *cawl* for the children. So this bread is to go with the *cawl*. And lots of tins from the Co-op – tins that have lost their labels, so the mothers' soup kitchen are having them for nothing. Beans, peas, maybe potatoes."

"Yes, so a surprise?" Pietro takes a tin without a label out of the box and shakes it next to his ear. "Hello? What have we here? Rice pudding, maybe? Or strawberries? We can't be putting strawberries and rice in the soup. Keep it for pudding, maybe? But no! Very good, making food for the poor children is very good … That is like the houses at home in Bardi … Wait here …"

Pietro hesitates for a moment. He tosses his cleaning cloth back in the bucket and runs into the cafe. Through the glass, Guto can see him opening the door to go behind the counter and then he disappears through to the kitchen at the back. Before long he's back with Nina, his daughter, following. They each carry a box. He bustles through the cafe door and back out to Guto in the street.

"Here you are! Food for the mothers' soup kitchen. A bit of bread – it's yesterday's but it'll do for toast, yes? There's jars of jam that are opened, with some jam left. And apples. We've just had a big delivery of apples from Monmouthshire. Nina will help you carry them. Go now. *Presto, presto!* The children want their food ..."

He gives one box to Guto to carry on top of the one he has already, and says that Nina will carry the other to the chapel.

They are hustled off down the street by the Italian before Guto has a chance to make a to-do about thanking him for the food. As he carries his boxes, Guto takes a quick, shy look once more at the Italian girl walking alongside him. She glances at him at the same time and catches his eye. She smiles at him. He can do nothing but smile back.

He turns back to look at Bertorelli's. Pietro has resumed his window cleaning. Behind him, he notices Eira, his sister, going in through the cafe door. He looks at the clocktower of the hall. Probably going to buy her lunch, he thinks. He looks at the dry bread in the box in his arms.

The chapel vestry is a hive of activity. Benches and long trestle tables fill the main hall, where there is room for about two hundred children. Some of the mothers are busy laying out cups, bowls and spoons on a table under the kitchen serving hatch. At the back of the hall there is a small room full of steam and the sound coming from a huge cooking pot bubbling merrily. Guto goes over to his mother. Llew is sitting in the corner and Dewi is jumping on the empty cardboard boxes surrounding him.

"Take the bread and put it on the table over there by the hatch," his mother tells him. "That's where we'll be serving the *cawl*. The children will be coming into the hall, and picking up a bowl and spoon from the table over there, and someone will direct them over here then. They can get their bread after that. And who's this with you?"

His mother has only just noticed Nina. The Italian girl smiles, unable to reply to Beti's question in Welsh. Guto jumps in to bridge the gap.

"She's Nina, the daughter from Bertorelli's, Mam. Nina – *Mamma!*"

"Dear, dear, is that box heavy, Nina *fach*?" Beti says. "Put it down on the table here. What have you brought, then?"

"Mister Bertorelli, Nina's father, has given all this as a gift from the cafe," Guto explains. "Look, there are apples from them in my box."

"Goodness me, fair play to them."

"And jam. Look!"

"Oh, excellent – and thanks. Thanks, Nina. How do you say 'thanks' in Italian, Guto, love?"

"*Diolch* – Welsh; thanks – English ..." Guto gestures to Nina.

"*Sì, sì,*" she cottons on. "*Italiano – grazie.*"

"Gra ..." Beti stumbles.

"*Grazie*," Nina says.

"Gassie," Beti says. "*Diolch yn fowr iawn.* Thank you very much."

"*Grazie, molte grazie*," Nina says, understanding. "*Dio...*"

"*Diolch*," says Guto to encourage her.

"*Diolch*," she says.

The three of them smile at each other. Then Guto scoops the tins the Co-op have donated out of the box and puts them on a table beside the enormous stewpot.

"Ah! Could you open them for us to see what's what?" asks his mother, turning back to the stewpot and giving its contents a stir with a long-handled wooden spoon. A large bone surfaces.

Nina looks at the bone with interest.

"It's a marrowbone," explains Beti Lewis. "Not much meat on it but it gives the broth some flavour. Rees, the butcher in Bridge Street, it's him who's given us the bones."

"For free?" Guto asks.

"Oh, yes. The small shops are very happy to give us stuff for free. It's the big shops on Dunraven Street that are tight-fisted."

"But not Bertorelli's cafe," says Guto.

"No, fair play. Bertorelli's – *da iawn*. DA IAWN! VERY GOOD!" Beti Lewis says to Nina.

"*Bene!*" she replies.

"Where's the thing to open tins, then?" asks Guto.

"Over there – there's two or three over in that corner."

When Nina sees Guto opening two of the tins laboriously and clumsily, she reaches for another opener and opens a tin quickly and efficiently. It's clear that she's an old hand at such work.

"What have you got in the tins," Beti asks.

"Potatoes in this ... pears ..." and, looking into Nina's tin, "... peas!"

"Peas!" says Nina. "*Piselli!*"

"Put the fruit in this big bowl here," Beti says, "and bring anything we can add to the *cawl* beside the stove here. The bones need to simmer for about another hour yet. Then we can put in the vegetables. The children will start arriving around three, after school."

The tin-opening goes on for a while. Beti Lewis grows concerned that she is keeping the girl from her work. She mimes looking at a wristwatch, points towards the street, and points at the girl.

"Bertorelli's?" she asks, raising her eyebrows and opening her hands.

"*No, no,*" Nina says, shrugging her shoulders unconcernedly. She turns back to her tin-opening.

A short while later, the group in the kitchen sense a silence in the main hall. One of the other mothers goes to the serving hatch between the two rooms to see what's up.

"Beti!" she shouts. "I can't believe my eyes! Come here, quick – look!"

Beti rushes to her side and peers through the hatch.

"Well, bless the Lord and all his works," she says.

They can see that a woman carrying a huge plate loaded with home-baked biscuits has walked into the vestry. She is now walking up to the serving table under the hatch. It is Dilys Mainwaring.

"Dilys, Dilys," says Beti, tears in her eyes. "What in the world is this? You haven't buried poor Watcyn yet. You've got a funeral to arrange. And look at you, you've been cooking biscuits all morning."

Dilys places the plate down next to the tea plates.

"There's not enough here to give the children one each," says Dilys ruefully. "The people of this town have been so good to us. Bringing us sugar and flour, butter and eggs, like there's no tomorrow. The least we can do is bake a few biscuits."

Beti rushes out into the vestry hall and gives her neighbour a huge hug. There is no need for words. After a while, Dilys releases herself from Beti's embrace. She dips into the pocket of her coat and puts half a pound of tea on the table.

"I expect there'll be some who'll welcome a hot cup of tea," she says. Then she turns and walks back towards the door leading to the street.

Work goes on in silence in the two rooms for a while after that. Before long, all the tins have been opened and suitably distributed.

"Oh, that's good," says one of the other mothers. "There's a fair amount of vegetables for us to put in the *cawl*. There's nothing worse than watery *cawl*."

"We won't see *cawl* like this for long, don't you kid yourself," says a much older woman. "As the strike wears on, the *cawl* gets thinner."

"And there's a good selection of fruit in the bowl as well," another remarks.

"Today's *cawl* could do with some fresh herbs," says Beti Lewis. "Guto, could you go to the People's Allotments? As it's the end of the summer, maybe some of the men are up there clearing the plots. Maybe you could get some fresh leaves. Parsley would be good."

"Will do, Mam," replies Guto, carrying the empty tins to the bin.

"Oh, there's a good lad you've got there, Beti," says one of the mothers. "Takes after his father, does he? Is your Moc good around the house?"

"Good for nothing, like every husband who's a collier!" Beti says. "Every time I ask him to do something he'll most likely say, 'I'm naked and I'm in the bath'!"

"Better than our Rhod," says another of the wives. "'I'm naked and I'm in bed' he says all the time!"

The women's laughter rings round the kitchen and Nina smiles too, to see the relief there.

"Nina *fach*," Beti says, and puts an arm round her shoulders. "Thank you so much, you're such a good girl. Diolch ... How do you say it, again? Grassi ..."

"*Grazie!*" says Nina, smiling.

"Off you go now, and take a couple of Dilys' biscuits." She takes two biscuits off the plate and gives them to the girl. "No one in the Rhondda makes biscuits to match Dilys Mainwaring's!"

The girl tries to refuse the biscuits, pointing at the empty tables where the children will sit.

"No, you deserve it, *grotan*!" Beti presses them on her and gives her an exaggerated wave.

"Yes, say thank you to Bertorelli's cafe!" says another.

"Fair play to the Italians," someone else chimes in.

Chapter 10

Up in the People's Allotments, two or three people are tending their plots. Clearing off the plants that had yielded the summer's crops is the main activity. There are smoky bonfires here and there.

The valley looks different from up here. Guto can see that it looks very beautiful from this distance. Because of the strike, there isn't much smoke rising from the coal mines' chimneys. The rows of terraced houses are like a fish skeleton – two or three rows running at the same angle, then the pattern changes as the buildings follow the contours of the slopes that make Cwm Rhondda very narrow just here. There is a smattering of coloured bricks, around windows and chimneys, in some of the terraces, and the grey-blue roofs of north Wales slate catch the light here and there.

Guto can see the railway and the narrower tramways, like snakes between the works and the various waste tips. The valley seems quiet. The bracken on the hillsides is the sharpest colour today, not the black of the mines. That afternoon, one could almost say that the mountains had taken the valley back from the miners.

Over in the highest corner of the allotments, he spots Gwyn. He's busy raking together old bean and pea stalks into a heap.

"How's it going, Gwyn?"

"Hello, lad! Am I pleased to see you. You couldn't give me a hand with this pile, could you?"

"You want to burn it, do you, Gwyn?"

"No, carry it. There's some old sacks in that little shed. Go and fetch them, there's a good lad."

"Carry it where?" Guto asks, when he returns with the sacks.

"To the ponies," Gwyn says, starting to stuff the green stems into one of the sacks.

Guto follows his lead and fills another sack.

"The ponies on the mountain, Gwyn?" Guto knew that, when the winter started to bite on the tops, wild Welsh mountain ponies sometimes came down from the Brecon Beacons.

"No, no, in the pit, lad! The ponies are still in the mine, don't you see?"

"Ah!" The penny drops. Although the miners are on strike, the pit ponies that pull the wagons carrying coal from the face to the shaft are still in their stables at different levels underground. "How many ponies are there in the Pandy, Gwyn?"

"About two dozen, something like that. There's hay underground for them, but someone has to go down to put it in the racks in their stalls. And I'll be taking a cabbage or two for them. One of them, Prince, my pony is pretty smart. If he smells cabbage on the level as I come to work, he pulls on his chains and gets very excited until I've given it to him. I'll get no work out of him until he's eaten the lot."

By now they have two sackfuls of pea and bean stalks.

Gwyn goes up and down his row of cabbages and cuts two.

"The caterpillars have eaten rather a lot of holes in these," he says. "Prince will be pleased to have one and Sunshine can have the other."

Guto watches him push one cabbage into each sack.

"How will you get these sacks down to the ponies, then, Gwyn?"

"Oh, everything will be fine, you know. We have an understanding. All the hauliers gave them a good feed yesterday, and then the officials let us take in the same to them at the end of the afternoon. We have to look after the ponies, you see."

"Wouldn't it be easier to bring them out of the pit?"

"Maybe that's what'll happen in the end. There's a little field available on the valley bottom next to the river, behind the Methodist chapel. We can get them up in a harness in the cage and take them out to the field. It's a bit of a to-do, mind. And, poor things, they're not used to the daylight."

"It'll blind them, won't it?"

"Yes, indeed. These ponies are practically blind in daylight. But that's what's strange – you'd swear they can see as plain as day down in the blackness of the pit."

"What do you mean, Gwyn?"

"Well, say a tram in the pit has run out of control, and has broken free of the brake shoes, the pony will know that and will stand or move out of the way before you've even heard it. And then, the pony will sometimes stand stock still on the rails when it's supposed to be pulling an empty tram or one full of coal. It doesn't matter how much you berate and encourage it, it won't budge an inch. Then, you realise why. There'll be a roof fall on the level some twenty yards in front of you. Roof timbers and pit props smashed like matches and tons of massive rocks in the fall. Oh, yes, the ponies can see well in the dark. That's why I take the sacks to them, you see."

"Oh, yes, Mam was asking, Gwyn ..."

"Yes, what is it, *crwt*?"

"They're making *cawl* in the kitchen of Ebenezer. Do you have anything to give it a bit more flavour?"

"*Cawl* for the children. Oh, I know what. I've got chives at the end of the row down there."

He takes his pocket knife and cuts several handfuls of the slender, green chives and puts them into a paper bag which he pulls out of his jacket pocket.

"There's nothing healthier than chives like this, ahead of the winter," says the old gardener. "They get a second wind after the summer and they'll crop well again. There'll be a lovely flavour to the *cawl* after you've chopped this up fine and put it on top of the *cawl* just before serving it to the children."

With a sack each over their shoulders, Guto and Gwyn walk down through the allotments towards the path that leads to Gelli-fawr. From there, Gelli Road takes them straight down to Dunraven Street.

Guto leaves the sack beside the entrance to the Ebenezer vestry and takes the chives in to his mother.

By now the big vestry is full of schoolchildren eagerly awaiting their hot meal.

"We only need to chop these up finely and then we'll be ready to move over to the hatch to start serving," Beti says.

"Yes, but you're not lifting that heavy vat!" cautions one of the mothers.

"No indeed," says another of the women. "Not with that bump in front of you! You do know you shouldn't be lifting heavy weights, don't you?"

Guto picks up his sack once more and walks on with Gwyn, past the Adare pub and the smithy, to the gates of the Pandy Colliery. All the way to the mine, wherever they pass a terrace of houses, Guto notices that all the front doors are open. On most doorsteps sits a miner. Although there are no work clothes to wash or dry because there had been no one on shift in the mine for the last twenty-four hours, there is a fire in every house. There has to be a fire for the women to cook. The house is too hot to sit inside, as it's a gorgeous afternoon.

What a sight, Guto thinks. Hundreds of workers lounging on their doorsteps, with the sun on their faces instead of coal dust. Many of the valley children are sitting on window sills, keeping their fathers and older brothers company.

At the gates of the Pandy there are about twenty miners picketing.

"*Shwd mae, bois?*" Gwyn greets them. "It's quiet, it is."

"Yes, there's been no bother here," replies one of the pickets.

"Did you have the policemen here? There were some over at Pen-y-graig."

"No, they didn't come here," answers another, "but we

saw some of them go over the White Bridge. Probably heading for the station in Tonypandy."

"Everything must be sorted in the Ely, then," says Gwyn.

Guto looks about, but there is no sign of Wil or his father.

"Who's your butty here, Gwyn?"

"Moc Lewis' son. Wil Wallop's brother. He's fetching a sack for me to the ponies. Who's looking after the gates on the inside?"

"Ray the Beak. He's been back and forth keeping an eye all day."

Gwyn puts his fingers to his mouth and gives a sharp whistle across the yard.

"Oi, Ray. Come here. This is to feed the ponies with." He turns to Guto. "Leave your sack by the gates. Ray can carry it so he can say he's done something useful today. Thanks, *byt*. I'm going underground now."

"By God, you'll get more sense out of the ponies than we get out of the donkeys that run the pit, Gwyn!"

"Yes, pit ponies. That's what we are too, *bois*. The pit ponies of the British Empire!"

Before he lets Gwyn go, Guto has a question for him.

"You just called my brother Wil Wallop. Why is he called that, Gwyn?"

"Oh, it's nothing. You know how colliers are with their nicknames. About a year ago, he gave some big lump from Merthyr who was trying to bully him underground a hell of a wallop, that's all."

* * *

Back in the cafe kitchen, Nina had eaten one of the biscuits she had been given in the vestry, with her afternoon coffee. She has brought another home to show her parents. She cannot stop talking about the spirit of the women she had seen in the vestry.

"Oh, this is tasty!" says her mother, eating the biscuit, adding in Italian that it's the best thing she's eaten since Christmas!

"Can I have a little bit?" asks her father and, after biting off a corner, he has to agree that it tastes exceptionally good.

Just then there comes a knock at the back door of the cafe. Nina is shocked to see a policeman standing there. A policeman with three stripes on his arm.

"*Papà! Papà!*" she calls.

"Good afternoon, sir, come in, come in ..." says her father, as if the policeman is expected.

As English is the main language of the Catholic school in Tonypandy, which Nina has starting attending, her understanding of the language is improving. But her father and the police officer have gone to a corner of the kitchen and she cannot hear their conversation.

Over there, the sergeant's deep voice comes in short sentences and Pietro's lighter voice answers.

"*Sì, sì – no problemo ...*"

Eventually the sergeant nods and turns to go. "*Ciao, brigadiere di poliza,*" Pietro says as he closes the door carefully behind him.

After the policeman has left, Nina is dying to know what it's all about.

"Oh, it's about the cafe, business stuff!" her father says. He turns in the doorway to the cafe. "What was the name of the lady who made the biscuits today?"

"I don't know," says Nina, "but Guto will know."

Pietro raises a finger and taps his forehead, making a mental note. Then he returns to his work behind the counter.

* * *

On his way back from the Pandy Colliery, Guto decides to follow the path alongside the river Rhondda. Between the smithy where the ponies are shoed and the bridge there lies a small, triangular field. This must be the field Gwyn was talking about, he thinks. This is where the ponies will be kept if they're brought out of their stables deep underground.

He thinks about the ponies. Underground, pulling heavy loads ... the same work, the same journey, every day ... What was it the collier at the gates of the Pandy had said? That was it – pit ponies of the Empire! Smart London trains and big liners to America wouldn't move if it weren't for the men of Cwm Rhondda – and many other valleys in Wales – crawling on their hands and knees in the dark and the pools of water to hack coal from the rock.

Guto walks on under the bridge by the church and turns up towards the backs of the buildings lining the main street. Ahead, he can see Ebenezer chapel on the other side of the street and he knows there is a gully along the side of the Cross Keys that goes up to the backs of the street and will bring him out at his home.

As he passes the back yard of the pub, he hears shouts and groans coming from the old stable. The building has no windows, but the upper half of the door is open. Voices of men, rough voices reach his ears, some shouting as if in encouragement and support. Guto's curiosity takes over.

As he approaches the stable door, he can see a gang of miners there. Judging by their voices, he reckons some have been in the pub a while. One or two wave their arms. Their attention is fixed on something against the far wall, and they all have their backs to the door.

Guto peers over the lower half of the door. He can see that a rope has been positioned across the far part of the building to create a square. He realises what is happening. The two men in the square have their fists up. They are boxing! They are pummelling each other!

He knows that there is a lot of fighting like this in the area. He had heard of tournaments being held in an old cemetery far down the valley, or sometimes staged up on the mountain as the dawn breaks. Heaven forbid that a policeman should come across such a fight. Bare-knuckle boxing is illegal ...

One boxer's face is covered in blood. It looks as if his nose is broken and one of his eyes is closing under a purple swelling. But he is not submitting. He holds his bare fists up in front of his face. He moves back and then to the side, trying to dodge the fists coming for him. The attacker, who has his back to the door to the right, turns and piles in, fists flying. His opponent crumples to the ground. A cheer goes up from the crowd. Guto notices the stocky man with the scarred face who was present at the meeting in the Empire. He is beside the post that holds up the rope in front of the crowd.

And then Guto sees the face of the victor. He is bloodied too, but recognisable still. His brother Wil.

He hears a voice from the centre of the crowd.

"What a knockout blow, Moc. This *crwt* of yours is shaping up!"

Chapter 11

It is three days after Watcyn Mainwaring's funeral, and Pietro is walking along Eleanor Street looking for Number 24. When he locates it, he knocks and waits for an answer.

Dicw opens the door. Pietro remembers him – Guto's friend. That makes it easier for him to shake hands and offer his condolences. Hundreds of people have called round to do the same thing, so Dicw is used to the formalities by now. He promptly invites Pietro into the house and into the kitchen.

Once he has expressed his condolences to Dilys and placed a gift of an Italian cake on the table, Pietro has a proposal to make.

"Our Nina was given one or two of your biscuits in the chapel," he says. "She had been helping with food for the children. Oh, such a biscuit, Mrs Mainwaring! I tasted a bit of it in our cafe. There's nothing like it in Italy!"

"Yes, yes," says Dilys. "I'm from Carmarthenshire originally and that biscuit recipe was my mother's. She was an excellent cook. She never gave anyone a cup of tea without a biscuit. Would you like a cuppa, Mister Bertorelli?"

"No, no!" he raises his hand to stop her. "I'm a cafe owner, remember! I get cuppa after cuppa all day. And that's why I'm here, Mrs Mainwaring. I'd like to sell your biscuits in the cafe. I'd like to buy your biscuits … We can pay you twopence a dozen. What d'you say?"

"Twopence a dozen?" echoes Dilys. "Every twopence would be very welcome now there's no wage coming into the house. How many biscuits would you want, Mister Bertorelli?"

"Six dozen a day, starting tomorrow?"

"Tomorrow! Six dozen ... Twopence a ... twelve ... a shilling! A shilling a day. That will be a huge help ..."

"Can you bring them to Bertorelli's by nine tomorrow morning?"

"Definitely. Oh, thank you very much Mister Bertorelli, sir."

"No, no 'sir'. Everything is as it was before."

"No, it's not as it was before ..." says Dilys.

* * *

"Strike pay tomorrow!" says Alun, rubbing his hands together. In the kitchen of Number 17, he has a smile dancing in his eyes.

"Well, even a great mountain of a Cardi like you won't get a great mountain of money, anyway," says Moc. "It'll only be a few shillings."

"Even a few shillings is a fortune for a Cardi," Alun says. "Back on our smallholding, we didn't even have the money to put coal on the fire. No, we had to cut peat up on the mountain and dry it in the summer, and then make a stack of it by the house to use in the winter. Coal grows out of the ground down here, for goodness' sake – you don't know you're born!"

"Give it a rest," sighs Beti. "Stories about how hard it is on you Cardis could keep us going until tomorrow morning."

"They're true, every word," Alun says, turning his chair towards the fire and warming to his subject. "Mam would fetch a swede from the field, you see ..."

Llew is sitting beside the chair, listening closely to the storyteller.

"So that's what we'd have Monday night, Tuesday night and Wednesday night – swede soup. One swede for the whole family for three nights. By Thursday night, the swede soup would be starting to get a bit thin. So Mam would go out to the field and fetch a saucepanful of snow, and put that in with the soup for Thursday night. Then, she'd cut our toenails before we went to bed."

"Why did she cut your nails?" Llew asks.

"After we'd gone to bed, you see," says Alun, pausing for dramatic effect, "she would put the clippings into the soup. And you know what? The best soup of the week was Thursday night's!"

Llew's jaw drops. Then he starts to laugh. One giggle swells until he is rolling on the floor, clutching his sides. Then he's out of breath and having a coughing fit. In no time at all he's doubled up, with his head between his knees, coughing jaggedly, his face flushed and purplish.

His mother rushes over and lightly slaps his back, then straightens his legs and tries to get him to breathe slowly and deeply and evenly. Gradually, the boy comes round. "Well, little man," says Alun, "are you alright, Llew *bach*? Oh, and I thought you'd had a pretty good week."

"Yes, he's been much better since we've had no work clothes drying in front of the fire," says his mother.

"That's one good thing about the strike, then," Alun says. "The house must be healthier for these little ones, mustn't it?"

Dewi comes over and sits on the floor, tucking himself into the crook of his brother's arm. Llew lifts his arm and put it on his brother's nape, and then round his shoulders.

"I'm taking Llew upstairs to bed," Guto says after a while. "He's tired out!"

The front door opens and Moc and Wil come into the kitchen. Wil settles on his haunches beside the fire and Moc makes himself comfortable in the second fireside chair.

"Did you go over to the Institute?" Alun asks.

"No, we went up the mountain."

"Bit of a walk," Wil says.

"Have you got a cut on your ear?" asks Beti, scrutinising Wil.

"Where?" Wil touches his left ear. "Oh, this. A hawthorn on the mountain …"

"The branches were over the path, you know," Moc replies just as quickly.

"What were you doing up the mountain, then?"

"Looking at the old levels where they used to mine." Moc is ready with a quick reply once more.

"Old levels?"

"Yes, we might need to go and dig coal for the house if the strike goes on for a while," says Moc, now with a bit of authority in his voice. "There won't be a monthly delivery of coal from the Pandy to every miner's house while we're on strike. And we need coal, don't we? Everything revolves around the fire – water for washing clothes, drying, cooking ..."

"Yes, I understand that full well," says Beti.

Moc stands up and pulls a few coins from his pocket.

"One shilling and threepence," he says, dropping it into the jug on the high shelf.

"Where on earth did that come from?" Beti asks.

"I won it playing snooker down the Institute," says Moc, rather lamely. "We were playing for a penny a game, and I got a good little run of games at the end of the afternoon, didn't I, Wil?"

"Yes, you did," says Wil fervently.

"You won at snooker?" Beti says incredulously. "From what I've heard, there's a good chance that our Llew would beat you playing with a broom handle! Was this before you went up the mountain or after?"

"Before ..." Moc says.

"After ..." says Wil simultaneously.

"Yes, well my rent money will be in the jug tomorrow," Alun says. "Once the Fed has paid out the strike pay. What time are they distributing it in the Institute?"

"Nine in the morning," answers Moc. "But you can bet there'll be a queue forming by eight. Money's tight in many houses already ..."

"True enough," Alun says. "But I've got a ha'penny in my pocket for tonight and I've only got to pay my rent tomorrow, so I'm going to wander down to Bertorelli's for a pot of tea and to see who's about. Ouch!"

He hits his head on the high shelf above the fire as he stands up.

"It's alright for some – swanning off down to the cafe!" laughs Moc. "It's a good thing you're a single man, Alun the Ox! But it's also a pity your head is so far from your feet!"

"I count my blessings every day," says Alun, going out through the kitchen door as Guto returns downstairs.

"That was a cruel thing to say, Moc," says Beti icily, "that he's a single man ..."

"I was only pulling his leg ..."

"Some wounds remain open, you just remember that."

"What d'you mean? Oh ... oh ... oh, yeah ..."

Wil raises his head and looks at his father.

"Am I missing something?"

"It's a while back ... it's why Alun came to the Rhondda to look for work in the mines in the first place," his mother explains.

"Yes, I remember him arriving here," says Wil, "but I was young at the time."

"You were all too young to understand at the time," Moc says. "Alun had just buried his beloved. A young woman from New Quay. Consumption."

"That's TB. She died of tuberculosis. Consumption," Beti says. "Those names fill me with dread. That disease crawls through our houses, flourishes in the smoke and the damp air and fills the lungs with little scars. And in the end, the lungs fill up with fluid and the poor patient can't breathe."

"They were supposed to marry," says Moc. "But the funeral happened before the wedding could. Alun couldn't face working on the smallholding afterwards. That's why he came here. Straight down the pit to forget."

"But he goes home every summer?" Wil says.

"Yes, yes. That's what he does. He keeps money by for his parents and he gives a helping hand at harvest time. But he doesn't have it in him to put down roots."

"He's a lovely man," Beti says. "But he's never had a sweetheart since he came here ten years ago. Women are hard to come by in the Rhondda, I'll admit, but Alun would be a good catch for any *crotan*, I can tell you that."

"Oh, we all know you think the world of him, Beti," Moc says, slightly scornfully. "That's his choice. But if he doesn't want a sweetheart and a family, well so be it."

"It's not his choice that he's got a broken heart, that's all I said," Beti replies.

They hear the front door open and close again.

Eira walks into the kitchen.

"And speaking of the Rhondda *crotan*, here she is!" Moc says with a smile.

"What are you saying about me, then, you rotten things?" says Eira as she walks to the fireplace and reaches for the jug.

She shakes it and hears the money jingling.

"Hooray, there's something in this jug at last!" She tips the money into the palm of her hand and lifts the jug back towards the shelf.

"Careful now!" calls her mother. "That money's for the whole family ..."

"But I haven't got any money to buy food! I can't be expected to work all day with nothing in my stomach!"

"The *crotan* is right," Moc says. "She's the only one working in this house at the moment ..."

Beti raises her voice. "Oh! So raising children and keeping house and making food for eight isn't work, is it not?"

"She's on her feet for hours in that shop," Moc clarifies. "You know what I mean ..."

"When did you last put anything into that jug" Beti asks Eira, catching hold of the hand which is holding the money before she can slip it into her pocket.

"I put in what I can," Eira answers unconvincingly.

"And where did you get this?" Beti is staring at her hand.

"What now?"

"That ring!"

Everyone looks at the ring on one of the fingers of Eira's right hand.

"That's Mam's ring – your grandmother's. Where did you get it?"

"It was in a drawer upstairs ..."

"A drawer in our bedroom," says her mother.

"But no one wears it now. And it's coming to me anyway. I'm the only girl, so I might as well wear it. Where's the harm in that?"

"You could have asked," Beti says, stroking her swelling belly.

"But you're always busy ..."

"You could offer to help ..."

"And I have a life too, you know ..."

"It's pure gold, remember. And it means a lot to me. It's the only thing I've got to remember Mam by."

"She'll take care of it, Beti," says Moc from his chair. "You know that as well as I do." He looks up at the jug on the shelf. "And whatever else, that'll be nicely full tomorrow. There'll be enough in there for everyone in the house."

A rather awkward silence falls on the house.

Eira looks sulkily at the jug on the high shelf.

"But there's not enough for me!" she says crossly. "And I want to catch the tramcar down to Ponty."

"What will you do in Ponty, *crotan*?" asks her mother.

"What does any young woman usually do? That's where my friends all go on a Saturday night. Oh well, looks like I'll be taking my new shoes to Goodmans the Pawnbroker until next pay day."

"Buying on the never-never and then pawning them – that makes no sense at all!" her mother explodes at her.

Eira goes upstairs to change her shoes. No one sees her put her hand on Llew's forehead and kiss his cheek, but they hear the slam of the front door behind her.

"What's pawning, Mam?" Guto asks.

"Pawning is taking something you have that's worth money to Goodmans. Say you take those brass candlesticks over there, which have been in your father's family since they were farming up on the Beacons. Well, Goodmans will examine them and offer maybe a shilling for them. You'll be pleased to have the shilling at the time. And when there's a bit of a wage coming into the house, you'll miss the candlesticks and you'll go to Goodmans and buy them back, but you'll pay one and threepence for them that time. So, if you borrow to buy something and take it to the pawn shop, you're paying for it three times."

Beti picks up Dewi to take him up to bed.

By the time she comes back down to the kitchen, Alun is back and is standing with his back to the fire. Beti can see from his face that something is amiss.

"Spit it out," she says to him. "Tell me what's wrong."

"The strike," he says. "Dai Lend Me came into Bertorelli's straight from the Institute. We should have given a month's notice to the owners before we came out on strike. So Mabon says it's unlawful for the Glamorgan and the Cambrian to go on strike. The Fed won't give the colliers in those two pits strike pay if they come out on strike to support us."

Chapter 12

The next day the strikers meet in the Institute. The miners are there at eight o'clock in the morning, but instead of queueing for their money, they are listening to some speeches about the difficult decision ahead of them.

The strike leaders and Fed officials are gathered on the stage in the main hall. Dai Lend Me is the first on his feet.

"I don't understand! I don't understand! The owners don't give a month's notice to the miners in the Ely pit before saying they're going to sack all the workers, but we're supposed to give a month's notice before striking! The whole thing's crazy!"

Several of the others raise their voices in support, with many bellowing it. With head bowed, one of the Fed officials gets to his feet and clears his throat self-importantly until the hubbub has died down.

"Since the establishment of the Fed in 1898, we've made great gains for the miners. You must bear in mind that the pit owners of Wales have been very crafty. They formed the Monmouthshire and South Wales Coal Owners' Association in 1873 – over a quarter of a century before we had the Fed – and they schemed among themselves to keep the wages of the south Wales miners lower than miners' wages in the Midlands and in the north of England. They helped each other to break every strike, every time there was a dispute in any colliery. Improving the lives of the families here in the Rhondda and in the other Valleys is a long, hard battle. The Fed, under Mabon's leadership, got rid of that beastly thing – the Sliding Scale – whereby wages would rise when the price of coal rose and fall if the price dropped. And the masters played dirty: selling Welsh coal cheaply on the world market because then they knew they could pay the colliers lower wages. The Fed won the battle to get a set and secure wage for the miners. Then, two years ago, Mabon and the Fed succeeded in reducing the length of a shift to eight hours. Just think of that! Our grandfathers worked a twelve-hour shift underground. So that was a great victory for us. But in gaining that, we had to give way on some other issues. And this is one of those – having to give a month's notice before striking. Mabon had no option but—"

"And where is he, Lord Mabon?" shouts someone from the floor.

Dai Lend Me is back on his feet.

"We got a set wage – yes. But is it a fair wage?"

"No! No!" shout several voices from the crowd.

"And that's the fight now. A fair wage. We can't work for less and less money. They're reducing the wages lower and lower – and we want a fair wage to live on. The minimum fair wage that a family can live on – that's what we want. We live in the richest valley in the world in terms of what it produces, yet we families are eternally poor."

"That is what we're all fighting for," says the Fed official. "But we have to stick to the rules. You can't come out on strike without strike pay from the Fed. Those of you in the pits the masters haven't closed must carry on working for now, then arrange a mass meeting and a proper ballot. There must be a vote in every pit and it must be taken one step at a time. The miners from Pandy Colliery, and the Ely and Nant-gwyn will be paid by the Fed, of course, because the masters have closed those pits."

"Will Mabon be at the mass meeting?" someone shouts from the floor.

"I give you my word he will. He'll leave his work in London and come all the way here. He's as good a man as ever stepped in shoe-leather."

"He'll be coming by train, though!" another yells. "He's too fat by now to be stepping anywhere!"

"Steady on, comrades," says the Fed man. "We mustn't turn against our own people. Mabon has worked tirelessly for many years on behalf of the miners of this valley. He deserves better than to be vilified like this."

The barracking gradually subsides.

"We'll call a meeting in the Empire on Friday evening, 16th of September at seven o'clock," announces the Fed man, after a quick consultation with the others on the stage. "Mabon will be there and he will address you. I now, with the approval of my colleagues around the table here, urge each and every one of you to start working your shifts again from Monday morning onwards."

The miners are very disgruntled as they leave the hall.

"Another strike falls flat on its face," says the miner with the scarred face.

"A month's notice! Who was the clown that agreed to such a thing?"

"Well, I'd better tell the missus to choose which set of clothes I'm supposed wear on Monday morning!"

"At least there'll be less to occupy the boys in blue," says another, nodding at a row of policemen on Dunraven Street, standing watching them.

Word had got round the grapevine very fast. This is a decision that would affect every shopkeeper. Along Tonypandy's main street there are over sixty shops selling all manner of goods – a grocer's shop, a butcher's, a fruiterer, a fishmonger, shoes, clothes, ironmongery, household goods, furniture, a pharmacy, and more high-class businesses such as a jeweller, a photography studio and even an electrical goods dealer. When the wages of the thousands of miners in the area were good, the shops did good business. The strike was not to their liking either. The fact was that a prolonged strike could mean businesses running into debt, and even being bankrupted.

A number of those shops' proprietors stood outsides the Institute as the miners left. Each one of them has a smile on his face. But the strikers file past them with heads bowed, giving them the odd surly glance.

Guto and Dicw come face to face with some of the miners as the men make their way back to their terraced homes. It was Dicw's turn to take his mother's biscuits down to Bertorelli's cafe that morning and he was carrying a large wicker basketful.

On the corner of Tonypandy Square, in front of the Empire, just before they turn down the narrow gully that runs behind Bertorelli's, stands a tall, white-haired man wearing a grocer's brown apron. Guto recognises him at once. It is Wilkins, the owner of a shop on the main street. It is to him that his mother pays rent for Number 17, Eleanor Street.

"Lewis Junior!" growls the shopkeeper as the boys get closer.

Guto frowns at being greeted in this way. He can't remember the shopkeeper ever speaking to him. Wilkins usually spoke only to other shopkeepers' wives, or the wives of local councillors, or those of the senior colliery managers. Guto looks at him and can see a threatening look in his eyes.

"You have been shopping at that Co-op cowboy outfit! What have you to say?" Wilkins bawls in English.

"Yes, I have carried—"

"You admit it! You bold rascal! Have you no sense of guilt at all! It's not even a proper shop – it's owned by the people and they don't run it as a genuine business should be run!"

"They offered—"

"Oh, yes! I'm sure they offered you your groceries at a bargain price and 'take them now and pay as you can' and all that. As well they may: they don't have overheads as I have. You'll have me in the poorhouse. I want a word with your mother."

"She is in the chapel—"

"Oh, a good Welsh chapel lady, your mother is. Yes, we all know that. But she's also good at breaking contracts. I, as the house owner, had her sign an agreement that she buys all her groceries at my shop on Dunraven Street—"

"She does—"

"Don't interrupt me, boy. She has broken her contract with me and that has serious consequences. Tell her to call in at my office at the back of the shop this afternoon at two o'clock sharp!"

And with that, the angry grocer turns on his heel and walks away down the pavement towards his shop.

"You'd better go home and tell your mother," Dicw says.

"That man doesn't understand the thing at all," says Guto. "That wasn't shopping for home, but taking the food the Co-op had given us for free for the children's soup kitchen in the vestry."

"I know that," Dicw says. "But he has totally misunderstood. Hadn't you better go and tell her?"

"Mam's in the vestry preparing the food for this afternoon. I'm supposed to be there just now – to go to the Co-op to fetch more food."

"But you can't! What if Mr Wilkins sees you again?"

"There's nothing wrong with what we're doing – that's what's so stupid. He's had all this business from Mam buying food for the household – even though he charges her more than the Co-op. But we've got no choice but to go there."

"Do you want me to go and fetch the whole order from the Co-op to the chapel?"

"We'll see. Let's take these biscuits to Mister Bertorelli first, eh?"

"Ah! Welcome to the big men!" The Italian is as jolly and warm as ever. "Yet more of Dilys Mainwaring's lovely tasty *biscotti* for me. Very good. *Bene*! Nina. Nina! Come and arrange this basketful of *biscotti* on this big *piatto* here."

Nina appears, wiping flour from her hands. She smiles at Dicw as she accepts the basket from him. Guto thinks her smile broadens somewhat as she catches sight of him. The dark hair and those white teeth ... Had she really smiled more at him? Maybe it was just his imagination running wild, he thinks then.

He watches Nina transfer the biscuits from the basket to the platter, counting in Italian as she does so.

"*Sessanta... sessantuno... sessantadue...*"

The words and her voice are like music to Guto's ears. Eventually, she delightedly announces that there are definitely one hundred and twenty.

"*Centoventi! Molte grazie!*"

"*Uno momento!*" Pietro says. He goes to a small box kept in a drawer in the kitchen and extracts a shiny coin. "A shilling, one shilling to give to *Signora Mainwaring, per favore.*"

"Thank you very much," says Dicw as he receives the payment for the biscuits. "*Grazie!*"

Guto turns to Nina and, mostly by gesturing and pointing, succeeds in conveying his meaning to her.

"We're going to the chapel now – food – eating..." He mimes eating.

"*Cibo,*" Pietro translates for her. "*Mangiare.*"

"*A!*" Nina grasps the meaning. "*Cappella!*"

"Yes, yes – *sì, sì, cappella* – for the little children. The ... *bambinos!*"

"Oh, you are going to the chapel to prepare food for the little children, are you?" Pietro asks.

"*Sì, sì ... uh ...* yes, yes," says Guto.

"Very good, *bene*. But Nina cannot come with you today. Work calls!"

Guto nods to indicate that he totally understands. He shrugs his shoulders in sympathy with Nina.

"Very well, maybe see you tomorrow," Pietro says. "Busy, busy – *impegnato!* – see you in the morning – *ciao!*"

He closes the door behind them, but not before Guto manages to catch Nina's eye and give her another little smile before departing.

"He sees really busy today, didn't he?" observes Dicw.

"That's how he's been every morning for a while ... since the start of the strike, actually," says Guto.

"Since Mam started to make biscuits for him, maybe," Dicw says.

Yes, Beti Lewis does have a box of goods to collect from the Co-op she says, and yes, she fully understands that she will have to go and see Mr Wilkins at eleven o'clock, and yes, it would be fine for Dicw to carry the box from the Co-op but Guto would have to go with him because otherwise the shop staff won't give him the food. Beti says she will explain the whole thing about the soup kitchen for the poor children to Mr Wilkins, and would make him aware that all members of the Fed would be boycotting his shop if he were to threaten them like this again.

"Many tables in this valley are short of food," Beti tells the boys. "People will do all manner of things they wouldn't countenance before this happened – all to get something to put on the table for their children. So off you two go – and don't dawdle!"

They get the box with no trouble. Guto is well-known to the staff by now. They can't help pulling his leg.

"Goodness me, Guto *bach*. You must have gone weak all of a sudden. It takes two of you now to carry this little box that weighs nothing? Look! I can carry it one-handed."

"The poor things, Meri *fach*!" chips in another of the shop girls. "I'm sure there'll be three of them tomorrow!"

"Maybe the third will be a guard?" suggests the first girl. "Can't be too careful. There are wolves abroad in the streets. They've started eating each other in Cwm Clydach, or so I've heard!"

"Cheerio, boys!" Meri says. "Have you got a stick to keep the thieves at bay?"

After the boys leave the Co-op and are back in the main street, Guto gives a deep sigh. Who is walking up the pavement on the opposite side of the road but Mr Wilkins the grocer.

"Quick!" he tells Dicw. "Turn and look at this window!"

The pair turn their backs to the street and feign an interest in the goods in the window display. This of all shops! thinks Guto, as he realises that they're looking at women's clothes in the window of Elias Davies. Inside the shop he can see the proprietor scowling at the two of them. He can see him calling Eira over and saying something to her ...

"Hiding from me, were you, boys!"

They both jump, and turn to face Wilkins, scrutinising them with his eagle eyes.

"Or are you going to spend your strike pay on new skirts? Oh no, of course – there is no strike pay, is there!"

Wilkins carries on walking, with a spiteful smile on his face.

"At least he didn't say anything about the box this time!" Guto says. "Mam's burst his bubble as far as that's concerned."

Behind them the bell on the door of Elias Davies tinkles.

"He says he doesn't want you loitering in front of his window," Eira states. "You're hiding the clothes. You're putting customers off. He said …"

"Yes?" Guto says.

"He said that you stink and you should go home and have a bath …"

Chapter 13

"It brings we who are gathered here tonight great joy that there will be no strike in the Cambrian or the Glamorgan pits. No one improves their lot by striking, and everyone is the poorer ..."

Beti Lewis is listening to the minister of Ebenezer, the Reverend Edward Richards, address the congregation attending the Sunday evening service in the chapel. She and Guto are the only ones form Number 17 in attendance.

Each time she listens to a preacher in the pulpit, her mind goes back to her own father, the Reverend Robert Hughes, Merthyr Tydfil. It is many years since she's heard him preach but she can still recall his voice.

She also knows instinctively what his opinion would have been on any subject, and she knows how he would have presented the reasoning behind that opinion to the congregation. She turns her attention back to the Ebenezer minister.

"And if I may remind you, dear friends, of that about which I spoke in the monthly meeting of the Union of Pontypridd and Rhondda Welsh Independent Chapels held at Bethania, Gilfach-goch earlier this month. I was presenting my paper, 'The best way to preserve and foster the interest of young people in the work of the Church', and my offering was favourably received by the meeting ..."

My dad wouldn't have boasted about himself like this, thinks Beti.

"The text is a timely one, and it was clear from the discourse that was to be had over the refreshments, provided by the good ladies after the address, that this is a matter weighing heavy on the minds of today's religious leaders ..."

From the *sêt fawr* – the special, railed-off area where the chapel deacons sit – comes a cry of "Yes, indeed! Hear, hear!" One of the deacons is ostentatiously sucking up to Mr Richards. Afan Davies, the optician, thinks Beti. That one was forever decrying young people, and was in his element handing down punishment when their cases came before the court. Afan Davies was a Justice of the Peace, and Chairman of the Bench in Pontypridd. He strongly believed that, for justice to be served, magistrates should come down hard in the valley.

"It has become obvious that it is a completely misguided step on the part of the workers in mid-Rhondda to insist on coming out on strike without giving the masters the required notice. Respect must be shown to authority, and it's time to set aside reckless behaviour like this. I am pleased that the miners are prepared to listen to the words and the example of their leader, Mabon, who seeks reconciliation and peace. There is no sense or righteousness in the deeds of some hot-headed troublemakers who mislead the workers into throwing order to the wind and breaking the legal agreement with the colliery owner who puts bread on their tables ..."

Yes, and not much more than bread, and maybe a bit of cheese, Beti thinks. Her father would hardly have exalted Mabon, either. A man too fond of the sound of his own voice, according to him. Yes, he has a big voice, but empty vessels make most noise. Mabon often led the crowds of miners in hymn-singing to unite their voices if the run of an argument looked likely to lead to divisiveness. No, the old minister from Merthyr was a Keir Hardie man. Her father had admired this Scotsman who, by now, had been the Member of Parliament for Wales' capital of iron and coal for over ten years. If anywhere had seen the suffering and strife arising from industry, it was Merthyr. But Keir Hardie spoke out in the House of Commons time and again in the name of the workers, and huge crowds gathered to hear him speak at public meetings.

"What I said at the monthly meeting, and which is as true today as it's ever been, is that our young people should submit to God's divine order in this valley. There is a place for everyone. Put a mandrel in the hand of one man, put a Bible in the hand of another. We need the man who leads the blind pit pony, and we need the custodians of the collieries to direct the produce of the valley to the best markets worldwide so that money comes back here to be placed, ultimately, into the hand of the worker to support his wife and his children in his home ..."

There's not much in the jug on the shelf, Beti thinks. And when there is more in it, it's not there for long. It's gone in a flash.

On the way back up Gelli Road after the chapel service, she asks Guto what he'd thought of Mr Richards' words.

"He likes quoting himself, doesn't he?" is her son's only comment. Guto's grandfather wouldn't have done that, thinks Beti. He would be more likely to quote Keir Hardie.

"The managers attack the workers, the workers attack the managers. The system needs changing," she says aloud.

"What's that?" Guto asks.

"Your grandfather quoting something Keir Hardie said.

"Oh, I know – the man from Merthyr."

"Yes. He sees things for what they are. He wants the coal mines and everything else to be the property of Wales and the people of Wales, so he says."

"How would that work, then?"

"The money would come to the country and to the people and be shared between everyone; it wouldn't stay in the hands of a few."

"D'you think the owners would be willing for that to happen?"

"That's why Keir Hardie's in the House of Commons in London – sometimes you have to change the law of the land."

"But it's the law of the land that says the miners can't come out on strike."

"You're right. The law's on the side of the big masters at the moment. That's why David Thomas, the big pit owner round here, is himself an MP. He's looking after his own pocket, he is!"

Back in the kitchen of Number 17, Wil stands in the middle of the floor preaching in his own, unique way. But it is not the words of the Ebenezer chapel pulpit that are coming out of his mouth.

"I'm telling you! I saw the two of them going like thieves in the night round the back of the police station."

"Which two are you on about now?" Moc asks.

"The bloke from Bertorelli's ... what's his name?"

"Pietro," replies Alun, sitting on his haunches in front of the fire.

"And that girl, his daughter ..." Wil continues.

"Nina?" Guto asks.

"Yes. Them. Him – Mister Buenosera – carrying a big shiny urn and the little sen-yo-rita carrying an enormous platter with a cloth over it. Taking tea and biscuits to the cops through the back door, they were. There's lovely, isn't it? Policemen here to break the strike getting a cup of tea and a biscuit from the townspeople!"

"Well, there was no trouble with the policemen, Wil," says Moc from his chair. "Everyone saw eye to eye and respected each other. They were mostly Pontypridd lads."

"And I suppose everyone deserves a cup of tea," adds Beti, putting tea-leaves in the pot.

"But where's the spirit of unity in the valley?" blusters Wil. "Why don't the shopkeepers stand with the strikers?"

"Oh, you're expecting too much now," Moc says. "Remember, the main officials in the works are the main customers for many of the shops."

"And they're on the bench in the court ..." adds Alun.

"And in the *sêt fawr* in the chapel ..." says Moc. "And they own most of the houses we live in. They want to make sure we carry on paying the rent ..."

"A strike's bad for shop business too," Alun says.

"But really – giving food and drink to the police!" Wil cries again.

"The Bertorelli family have got to live too," Alun says. "These last few weeks there have been a lot of empty tables there."

"They're probably Dilys Mainwaring's biscuits." Guto interjects. "The cafe orders a load from her every day."

"And it's good for her to get that little bit of money," Beti says, as she passes on her way to the fire to scald the tea.

"That's the point," Alun says. "The poor are glad of anything. If rich people could pay the poor to die in their place, the poor would make a tidy living."

"But why can't we pull together?" Wil's voice has calmed down by now. He pushes his fingers through his hair and pulls his head back, squeezing his eyes shut as he does so. He shakes his head in a gesture of hopelessness.

"Have you had a nosebleed?" asks his mother, as his nostrils face her.

"It happens now and again."

"Underground?"

"No ..."

"You need to spend more time down the pit," she says. "You have fewer accidents down there, believe it or not."

The conversation ends as everyone drinks their tea. Beti fetches Moc's and Wil's work clothes and places them in front of the fire.

"It'll be odd having these back all mucky and wet again tomorrow afternoon," Beti says. She turns to Alun. "I'll get your clothes out during the day tomorrow. How long d'you want to sleep for before you go on night shift tomorrow?"

Since the lockout Alun has taken to sleeping at night,

like everyone else in the house.

"Might as well sleep one more night in the chair down here before going back to the old system tomorrow night," Alun says. "I've promised to go up to the allotments to give Dic Tic Toc a hand. He's asked me to clear a little patch to plant leeks. It's the right time, he says, and you know how Dic Tic Toc is for keeping to time."

"I'm going with Dicw to see the recruitment manager in the Cambrian pit tomorrow morning," Guto says. "He's going to ask if he can start as a butty *bach* to load coal for Emrys, his grandfather. They need the money. His brother Edward has taken the place of Watcyn in the Pandy."

"Dilys is taking in washing, that's what I heard," Beti says. "I've a mind to ask her to do some for me. She'd lighten the load of the housework here ..."

"Why on earth would you do such a thing, woman?" Moc says. "We have a washtub out the back."

"And I don't have to go back to school this month, Mam," Guto says. "I'll be leaving in a couple of months anyway. I'll be more use doing a but of work around here before starting in the pit."

From his bed the following morning, Guto hears the hooters of the Glamorgan and the Cambrian and then the sound of hobnailed boots on the streets. He hears Llew coughing and Eira sighing exasperatedly and turning to face the wall. He hears his mother singing as she carries the bucketfuls of water. Nothing's changed, he thinks.

* * *

Dicw and Guto are back in Eleanor Street before nine. Dicw has a promise of work. Guto could see that the manager wasn't too keen, but he couldn't refuse. Dicw hurries to tell his mother the news that he'll be starting on the Wednesday morning shift.

There is a basket of biscuits on the table of Number 24. While the boys are there, a load of bedclothes arrive for Dilys to wash and she is glad of Dicw's help.

"It'll be odd after Wednesday without you here to work the 'dolly'," she tells him.

"Shall I take the basket down to Bertorelli's for you?" asks Guto.

It is with mixed feelings that he goes on his errand. What would his brother Wil think if he were to see him carrying a basket of biscuits that are going to end up in the hands of the police guarding the mines? On the other hand, he was looking forward to opening the back door of the cafe and seeing Nina.

"Ah! *Biscotti* Mainwaring!" says Pietro, welcoming him into the kitchen. The Italian exaggeratedly slaps his own forehead. "I forgot. *Che stupido!* How foolish of me – I didn't tell Mrs Mainwaring that the policemen have left Tonypandy. No need now for tea and *biscotti*!"

"Oh!" says Guto. "Do you want me to take these back to her?"

"*No, no,*" Pietro replies firmly. "Here's a shilling for you to give to Mrs Mainwaring. But very sorry, tell her. Bertorelli's cafe doesn't need *biscotti* after today. *Mi dispiace molto.* I'm very, very sorry."

Chapter 14

"Mam came into my bedroom to wake me at half past five, but there was no need. I'd been listening to the grandfather clock downstairs strike every hour since three."

Guto is over at Number 24 to hear how Dicw's first day had been.

"I went down in my nightshirt – it's an old one of Dad's – and got into my work clothes that had been warming on the guard in front of the fire all night. Edward was already dressed and it was a big day for him too, what with him moving from one pit to another. Mam had made a big pot of tea ready for us and it was waiting for us on the hotplate. Out the back to splash my face in the bucket of cold water. Then on with the vest and wool shirt, moleskin trousers with the leather belt, and then socks and hobnailed boots.

"Rinse out the three-pint tin jack, fill it, and stick the cork in. Into the kitchen. Mam had toasted some bread on a toasting fork. Then on with the jacket and muffler, and then my flat cap on my head. Water jack in my left pocket, tommy-box with bread and cheese in my right – and at that the hooter sounded, at the exact moment the clock struck six. Shoulder the shovel – Edward's shovel – from out the back, and out through the front. Edward was carrying Dad's mandrel and he was going up to the Pandy."

"You only had toast for breakfast, then?" Guto says.

"I was nervous. I didn't have much of an appetite. I'll tell you one thing: hearing the hobnailed boots reverberating off the street is a strange experience. I was a collier, Guto! Oh, it's such a shame Dad wasn't here to see me. But I got a big grin off Tad-cu when we joined up with him at his house on Kenry Street. On then past the Athletics Park and over to Clydach Road. It was half-light by now – a chilly morning, you know how it is in September, said Tad-cu.

"Past the spoil tip and the pithead buildings and then we're in the lamp room. I had to call my number through the little window and give the lampman there my tally as he handed me my lamp – it's Edward's old tally, number 367.

"Then into the cage shed. That's the entrance into the dark underworld. In we go to the cage and the banksman closes the gate. The banksman's already searched our pockets for fags or matches – stuff you can't take underground, you see, in case there's gas and it ignites. He gives the signal to the man who's doing the winding, he pulls a lever and – slam! – the doors closes and the cage descends. Dead slow at first, and then it picks up speed, the air is dusty and warm. Then it slows down and we land smoothly at the bottom."

"It was dark down there, then, was it?"

"Yes. The hitcher opened the gate and the examiner tested our lamps and then there's a mile to walk before we reach the coal face. Other colliers are splitting off here and there, going to their own places of work. We go into a hole in the wall and take off our jackets, mufflers and caps, and even our shirts. I grab my shovel and water jack and follow Tad-cu.

"The coal seam is ahead of us. It's shining in the light of

135

our lamps. Here it's about two feet thick. Tad-cu starts work – he uses the mandrel to hack the coal until it falls. I'm loading the coal into tubs that hold about a hundredweight each. Lifting the biggest lumps first – with my hands and arms ..."

Guto looks at Dicw's arms. He can see raw cuts and scrapes along their length. His hands, despite having been in the hot bathwater after returning home, are bloodied and there is still coal dust mixed into the angry flesh and under his fingernails.

"They'll harden up in about a week, that's what Tad-cu told me," Dicw says, looking at his hands. "The tubs then get shoved and dragged back towards the main tunnel and loaded onto the tram. That's my work then. Every tram carries about a ton.

"As Tad-cu cut deeper into the coal seam, he would put a wooden prop in every three yards or so. Tad-cu chewed tobacco all day, and every so often he'd spit the juice onto his hands. He told me to pee on my hands – that it would harden them!"

"Did you do it?"

"Yes, of course! I want hard hands, I do! And he told me to grow a moustache too. Apparently a moustache helps to keep the dust out of your lungs."

"But you don't shave yet, Dicw!"

"Well, I will be before long. And the I'll grow a moustache if I'm still working at the face."

"How many trams did you fill on the shift today?"

"Five. It was about seven tons. Tad-cu was pleased with

that – on my first day. Hopefully it'll be six tomorrow, he said.

"Half past ten, we had a bit of a break. The corner of the bread where my fingers held it was filthy – I ate the lot but chucked the crusts away for the mice."

"How many mice are there? Did you see any?"

"Yes, loads. Mice and rats. But there you go, it's them that keeps the pit clean."

"Clearing the crusts you mean?"

"Yeah, that, and what come out the other end!"

"*Ych-a-fi!*"

"Well, it's good they do that job, otherwise instead of a pit we'd have a cesspit and it'd stink."

"Three o'clock, we leave the face and leave the tools on the bar. The hauliers and ponies that pull the trams are ahead in front of us and their hooves raise the dust into our faces. The ponies are unharnessed and the hauliers take them to the stable, which is near the bottom of the shaft.

"Half past three, the hitcher is starting to count men into the cage. There's quite a gang of us now and they start chatting, pulling each other's leg and having a laugh. We come up in the second cage. The banksman opens the cage and it's lovely to feel the sun on our faces. But, of course, winter's ahead of us, Tad-cu said, and we won't see much daylight then. Across the yard to the lamproom and then the same journey back to town, in reverse. And that's the first day for you."

* * *

Before Dicw's hands start to properly harden, there is more excitement in the mid-Rhondda coal mines. Mabon is on his way back from London. The first meeting is in Cardiff – a Fed committee meeting on the Friday night and then a big conference with every pit in south Wales sending representatives to the Cory Hall in Cardiff. About two hundred and fifty members attend, representing almost 150,000 miners from across the south Wales coalfield.

That Saturday in Dunraven Street there are crowds of miners awaiting the return of the representatives on the train. Guto and Dicw stand in their midst and before long they hear a cry go up.

"There he is – Dai Lend Me! He's walking out of the station."

"We'll get to hear how it went now."

"Dai, what did Mabon have to say?"

Dai stands on the steps of the Empire so everyone can hear him properly.

"I haven't got much voice left, so please be quiet so I can say what I have to say once only. It was a stormy meeting, lads, and we had to shout to be heard."

"Has Mabon had a better offer from the Cambrian Combine?"

"He's probably sat with David Thomas, the owner, on the train all the way back to London!"

"I heard that they're big mates! The pair of them are members of parliament in London – that's how they are. Once they're the other side of Offa's Dyke, they forget where they come from."

"How can you have the leader of the Fed and the head of a mining company being as thick as thieves?"

"Him – David Thomas – will be Lord Rhondda before long – just you see!"

"Why do we have to go to London to solve problems in the Rhondda?"

Dai raises his hand.

"Can you pipe down for three minutes. Right. Mabon's first statement was this: 'My colleague David Thomas is not a well man. It will do his health no good to hear that the miners are out on strike.' That's what Mabon said!"

"Shame on him!"

"What about the health of this valley, then!"

Dai raises his hand once more.

"The next thing he said was, 'Half a loaf is better than none.' And a lad from Llwynypia said, 'We want every loaf that's in the bakery, *gw'boi*!' And then all hell was let loose! Mabon has had a better offer from the Cambrian Combine, he says, which is two shillings and threepence a ton for the tricky seam in the Ely. If you remember, it's two shillings and ninepence a ton we're asking for. No one wanted to accept the offer Mabon had. There's no point in further discussion with the owners, he says. So announce a strike in a month's time, we said. We had a vote and it was carried. There'll be a ballot now – a secret vote – in each pit. A lot of colliers in other valleys will join us in coming out. This, lads, is a battle for more than just a few pennies per ton. It's a battle for a fair wage that we can live on. That's what this is – a battle for a minimum wage. And the owners know that. So you'll hear more about the ballot at the start of the week."

A huge applause breaks out along the street – by now a dense crowd has gathered there. Another of the local leaders climbs up to the top of the steps.

"We're leading this time, lads. The MPs we have in the House in London don't understand the valley any more. In the past, they've come from parliament and told us how it's going to be. This time, it's different. We're telling them what we want. We're the ones that live and sweat in the valley, and understand the valley, and we are the ones who are telling parliament what's what."

There was another wave of deafening applause.

* * *

It is no surprise to anyone that the result of the miners' ballot is strongly in favour of striking. The date is officially set – the entire workforce of the Cambrian Combine in mid-Cwm Rhondda will strike from Tuesday 1 November onwards.

"There will be over eleven thousand miners from this area on strike!" says Wil from his place in front of the fire one evening, as they discuss what they face.

"And other pits in other valleys are bound to support us," Alun says.

"All the members of the Fed in south Wales are contributing out of their wages to give us strike pay," says Moc.

"But the owners are not taking this lying down," warns Alun. "I was reading in the Institute the other day that the

Monmouthshire and South Wales Coal Owners' Association is preparing. There won't be any mines that will be ready to pay a miner who's on strike in the Rhondda. And the pits that will still be working in south Wales are putting part of their profit per ton produced towards compensating the owners of the idle mines in the Rhondda."

"There's two sides to every big fight," Moc says. "We'll be ready for them come November."

Chapter 15

As September turned to October, the weather turned too. The usual Indian summer at the end of September pleased the gardeners on the hillsides and housewives with washing on the lines at the backs of the terraces below.

At the beginning of October came three clear nights, bringing a chill to the valley. There was frost on the roof slates and on the rough grass beside the paths to the mines. First light would reveal a thick mist hanging over the river Rhondda, slow to burn off. Only the hilltops rising above the valley were in view. After the cold snap, the wind turned round, pushing in heavy showers. Days of rain. Low, billowing cloud lies on the hills for days, weeping wave after wave of grey rain on the lives of the families in the terraces below.

The clothes on the line won't dry.

The workers' jackets are heavy and dripping by the time they reach their homes.

And, worse than all this, the rain runs into the mines and collects in pools in some of the tunnels. When the miners are below the coal seam to lever it free, they are lying in six inches of filthy water all day in places. Every butty *bach* has to fumble in black pools to retrieve the precious rock and load it onto the trams. There is no choice but to build up the fire with more coal and pile the wet clothes onto the fireguard in front of it. The house is filled with the damp smell of the pit.

Guto hears a change in the quality of Llew's cough. The hard bark coming from his chest turns into an unbearable wheeze at the end of every breath. He cannot relax into sleep and his face becomes paler and his eyes dimmer every day. Even little Dewi senses his suffering and offers his cup of water to Llew after a particularly draining bout.

Mid-month, one of the things that every family in the valley fears will happen to them, happens. This time it is the turn of Number 31, Eleanor Street. That was where Peg Leg Jac and his family lived. Guto had seen him hobbling along the street. He had lost a leg in a mining accident a few years back. There was no work for him at the mine after the accident, and he wasn't up to any other work in the valley either. He had received some compensation from the mine owner for his injury, but the family had been living on whatever they could scrape together since then. There were three children under ten years old in the family, and Mair, Jac's wife, worked all hours to bring in a few pennies to support them.

Everything of theirs that was of any value had already been turned into cash at Goodmans the Pawnbroker's. But by now that money had all gone. The family are starving and there is no money to pay the rent. Amidst the sound of the children's howls, Wilkins' men come to Number 31 and carry whatever furniture is left into the middle of the street. Then they padlock the door and take the key to Wilkins' shop. The family is left to the kindly compassion of this or that person in the street until someone in Gilfach Road says that there is an empty cellar in their house and that the family can move in there for a low rent, but no one must breathe a word to the owner of that terrace.

The following morning, Beti goes into her children's bedroom before going downstairs. She leans across Guto.

"Are you alright?" Guto asks, slightly unnerved by the change to her usual routine.

"Yes, but Llew's not well. He hasn't slept at all, he's just been coughing and coughing. Dear, dear, he's lathered in sweat." She reaches out her hand to Llew's forehead, then picks him up.

"Where are you taking him?"

"Downstairs. I'm going to give him a spoonful of paraffin to kill the germs and try and bring his temperature down."

"Let me carry him downstairs."

Guto takes hold of his brother and carries him down into the kitchen, with his mother following with the oil lamp. He sits down on the wooden chair, with Llew on his lap. Beti busies herself with fetching the jar of paraffin from the back kitchen and pouring some into a cup. She takes Llew and lifts a spoonful to his lips. Llew swallows the disgusting liquid without opening his eyes.

"There, there, Llew *bach*. This temperature's making you poorly, isn't it?"

She goes to fetch a blanket to put over him. His nightshirt is soaked with sweat from the fever.

"You *cwtsh* up here for a little while with your brother."

The bathtub and its cold water is already in the middle of the floor, ready for Alun's bath, and after filling the teapot for breakfast, Beti transfers boiling water from the boiler to the tub. Then she goes to the tap out the back to refill the boiler.

"My egg isn't in the saucepan on the fire!" moans Moc, after coming downstairs.

"I'm keeping it for Llew today," Beti says sternly. "He needs the nourishment. He hasn't been able to swallow properly for two days – he has a sore throat as well."

Moc leaves the house, grumbling, and Wil is silent.

When Alun gets home, he heads straight for the chair where Guto is nursing Llew on his knee and takes a look at the patient.

"He's worsening," he announces.

Alun first washes his hands in the tub and then opens Llew's mouth, holding his jaw down with one hand. He holds the oil lamp up to it with the other.

"Llew, listen to me now. Can you hear me?"

Llew makes a little noise in his throat.

"Put your tongue out. That's it, as far as you can ... Give me a big 'ahh' now ..."

"Aah ..."

"What can you see, Alun?" asks Beti.

"I'm looking at his throat ..."

"Yes ... and how's it looking?"

"It's very red ... it's swollen ... and that little dangly bit is red too ... and ..."

"And what?"

"There's ...there's a white crust there ..."

"Is that ... is that what I think it is?"

"Yes," Alun says. He closes Llew's mouth and straightens up. "Diphtheria. There's only one thing to do."

"But we'll never afford the doctor."

"You've got no choice. You have to take him to the Tyntyla Isolation Hospital in Ystrad. That's the law. The infection could go from one house to another all along the street. You have to keep him in isolation – it's the Local Board of Health rules."

"But he could ..."

"He'll get the best care there. Come on, I'll hurry now, and then Guto and I will carry him up to the hospital. It's about three miles, we can take turns in carrying him. Go and fetch some clothes now for him."

"Eira!" Beti shouts. "Look after Dewi!"

In less than ten minutes the four of them are leaving Number 17. Alun carries Llew in his arms for the first stretch. It's still dark, but at least it's not raining. Guto takes him once they reach Dunraven Street, where the going is level. Alun carries him once more from the railway bridge up the road towards the Glamorgan Colliery at Llwynypia. Guto sees the lights at the pithead where the last of the men are going down the shaft. Wagons are already on the move along the tracks. Then the pit suddenly disappears from view – a high and sturdy wooden fence has been erected between the road and the pit.

From the brick works, Guto takes over the carrying once more, past the football field and over the Rhondda bridge. Alun takes over for Tyntyla Road and Guto does the last little bit – uphill on a little lane that leads to the Isolation Hospital.

Guto feels as if they have a big, black cloud over their heads as they walk in through the door.

The nurses know immediately what needs doing and do it quickly and efficiently. In no time, Llew is lying in a little bed surrounded by curtains, having been given a warm bath and a change of clothes. The nurses have taken his temperature and one of the senior ones has shone a battery-powered torch down his throat to inspect it.

The diagnosis is confirmed. Beti sits down on a chair beside Llew's bed.

"I'll fetch him home with me when he's better," she says.

"You haven't had any breakfast yet," Alun says.

"Yes, I have. I had something before the men got up," she counters.

"No, you haven't, Mam," Guto says. "I was with you then. Remember?"

"Well, I don't want ..."

"You have to look after yourself, Beti," says Alun. "And the little one ..."

"What am I going to do with him?" Beti buries her face in her hands. She makes no sound, but her mouth is open in a silent scream.

Alun bends down and touches her arm.

"Give him enough water to drink and when he passes water, collect it in a bottle. There are enough of them in this place. Now, my sister caught diphtheria. But she got through it. It's true that children can die of it, but some get better. The advice an old lady in the village gave Mam was this – 'Collect the little one's wee, Mrs Jones, and with a little brush, paint her throat with her own wee.' And that's what she did. You stay here for the morning and Guto and I will go home to Dewi, so Eira can get off to work."

* * *

When Alun gets up at three o'clock in the afternoon, he catches Beti blackleading the range. It is a dirty job – using a rag to rub the blacklead onto the big oven to the left of the fire, then the metalwork of the fire itself and the fire irons to the right. Like every mother in the Valleys, Beti does this every day to keep the metal polished and the house shining. But by the time she's finished she'll be almost as filthy as a collier.

The bathtub is in the middle of the floor, ready for Moc and Wil. Two bucketfuls of cold water are in it already, and Dewi is having great fun making waves in it.

"Did Guto help you carry the tub and the water in here, Beti?"

"Yes. He's gone to read the papers in the Institute now. He's obsessed with the news and current affairs since you took him down there."

"There's so much for us all to learn. How was Llew when you left him?"

"His breathing was easier. The air's so clean and so dry in the hospital. He has enough room in his bed there – we're constantly breathing all over each other in this house."

"Did you get a little brush from one of the nurses?"

"Yes, I did what you said—"

Moc and Wil coming in interrupts them. While Beti tells them what's been going on, Alun carries the hot water in from the boiler.

"Get your wash quickly," Moc says. "We have to go and see someone."

Beti tries to find out what he means, but "it's nothing for her to worry about" is the only information that's forthcoming from him.

Beti goes to the jug and takes out some money.

"You supper's on the hotplate when you're ready for it," she says. "I'm going back to the hospital. Now, I don't know where you're off to but there's no one except me to go to the hospital, you understand? They're very strict there. It's a dangerous disease."

Once Guto is back to look after Dewi, she puts on her coat and goes out.

"We'll have our supper when we get back," Moc says. "Come on, Wil."

"If you're happy looking after the baby, I'll go to Bertorelli's for a little while," Alun says.

Moc and Wil don't have far to go. Down the hill to Dunraven Street and round the back of the pub. There, in the old stable, are two or three dressed for fighting. They are doing various exercises to stretch their bodies and loosen up their feet. The man with the scarred face that Guto and Dicw noticed is there too.

"Tal?" Moc calls to him. "A word?"

After he's instructed one of the lads, he comes over to the door to speak to father and son.

"Can you arrange a bout for Wil here?"

"No problem, Moc. 'Ee's tidy with 'is fists, your lad. We'll 'ave a couple o' roun's 'ere one night next week, is it?"

"No, a big one this time, Tal. Up on the mountain. Against one of the Gilfach-goch lads. What about Saturday afternoon?"

"Oh, I'm no' sure if Wil's ready for tha' yet, Moc. Big lads over Gilfach, like. Like bulls, they are."

"It's not size that counts in a fight, Tal, you know that. It's the size of the fight in the man that's important. And there's plenty of fight in our Wil. Llew, the little one, he's under the doctor, and we need money ..."

"Everyone in the valley needs money, Moc. Tha's why we're producin' so many boxers, isn'it. But I'll see what I can do. Wil 'ere's comin' on good ... pretty good, I'd say ..."

Chapter 16

"What do you mean, 'Mam's taken it'?"

Eira is holding the empty jug that had been on the mantleshelf.

"She needs it for Llew, in hospital."

"So where's the money for things I need?"

Guto looks at his sister as if he doesn't recognise her, marvelling at how she can be so hard-hearted at such a time.

"Why are you looking at me like that?" Eira asks sharply, sticking her nose in the air and gazing left to right. "I always put the money back. I only borrow it until I get my wages from the shop."

That's the trouble with being a brother, thinks Guto – you know without a doubt when you sister is lying. Her voice rises in pitch until it's no more than a squeak and she purses her lips into a circle that looks like a hen's back end.

A feckless hen, he thinks, and goes out to the back to fill the coal bucket.

By the time he comes back in, she's gone. He helps himself to supper and he's just sitting down to eat when Alun returns and helps himself to a bowlful of stew too.

"And I have something very special for you to drink with your supper!" Alun reaches into his jacket pocket, extracts a large bottle of Welsh Hills cherryade and places it on the table in front of him.

"Why do you want to waste your money on a bottle of pop, of all things, Alun?"

"But that's what's so great," Alun says. "It's a present. It didn't cost me anything, not a single brass farthing. Pietro had heard about Llew, you see. 'I'll just fetch a little something for the big man' he said. He's got a big heart, fair play to him. But it wasn't Pietro who came back to the table with this bottle but ...the girl ... what's her name?"

"Nina?"

"Aha! I knew you'd remember her name! And she remembered your name too, you young pup! 'Gu-to,' she said. She was almost singing it as she pronounced it. 'Gu-to – cherryade,' she said. And smiling – oh, she's one that could melt the coldest of hearts, I'm telling you."

Guto presses his lips together and lets out a heavy sigh through his nose.

"Have you finished? Can we eat now?"

"Give me a chance to fetch some glasses for us. I take it I can have a glass of Nina's pop for carrying it up here for you? Or is it you alone who may have it, touched, as it has been, by her hand?"

"Give over, Alun!"

Alun pours the pop into two glasses in a way that makes the bubbles fizz. He places one ceremoniously in front of Guto and stands behind his own chair, raising his glass as if offering a toast.

"Ladies and gentlemen, please raise your glasses. To Nina and Guto!"

Alun grins inanely and nods round the room with his

glass still held high, as if addressing hundreds of people. He then downs the red liquid in one go before sitting down in front of his supper and belching extravagantly as the bubbles hit his stomach.

"Oh, do excuse me! I'm feeling a little giddy after that champagne."

"It's only pop from Porth, not champagne."

"Ah, that's where you're wrong. Even a glass of plain water can turn into champagne if you receive it from the right person. You'll come to understand such things, Guto *bach*. You've got it all ahead of you, you lucky devil! Now, eat your supper and stop being so literal!"

Once it's quiet, and there is nothing to hear other than spoons scraping on bowls and the sound of the pair blowing on their hot stew, Alun remembers that he has another thing to tell Guto.

"The chips! I almost forgot amongst all that excitement about the darling Nina ..."

"Leave off now, Alun. What chips?"

"Pietro wants you to go down to see him, tomorrow. He wants to offer you some work every now and again."

"Doing what?"

"He can tell you tomorrow."

At ten o'clock the next morning, Guto is knocking on the back door of Bertorelli's cafe. Nina answers the door to him.

He opens his mouth to say something to her, but suddenly he's speechless.

"*Buon giorno*, Gu-to!" she says, with a sunny smile.

"Bwon joarno," Guto repeats, relieved that she's provided

him with words. "Bwon joarno, Nina..."

"Ah! Here he is, the big man!" Pietro appears from somewhere. "Come in, come in."

"Um ...thank you for the pop last night." Guto addresses Pietro first and then turns to Nina, and nods and smiles at her. "Thanks, Nina."

"*Buon giorno*, Guto," says Emilia warmly. She is standing by the stove, cooking.

"And how is your little brother?" Pietro asks.

"He's still very poorly."

"But he's in the best place for him," Pietro says. "Right then. Work. That's what I want. You've seen Aldo's cart outside, haven't you?"

"The ice cream cart?"

"Yes. How would you like to push it up the hill to the Athletics Park on Friday night? There's going to be a big workers' meeting there, isn't there? And I was thinking—"

"But it's the middle of October! And the meeting's not until half past four in the afternoon. No one will want ice cream—"

"No, no, Guto – not *gelato*! Have you seen inside the cart? There is a layer of wool between the wood inside and the wood outside. That is what stops the ice cream melting in the summer."

Pietro taps his forehead. "*Intelligente*, Guto – *intelligente*. Well, my *cugina* – my cousin – she has married into a family that have a cafe in Blaenrhondda. They sell good ice cream; no, not ice cream! – *gelato*! They sell *gelato* in the summer but in the winter they use the cart to sell hot food. Do you see,

Guto, the cart keeps cold food cold and hot food hot ..."

"Hot food?"

"Chips!" announces Pietro. "You'll see, Guto."

Pietro walks over to his wife and shows him a large, shining saucepan. He lifts the lid to reveal a wire basket inside it.

"Emilia has a chip pan now!" He bends down to open one of the kitchen cupboards.

"You see these metal boxes? There's a lid on each one, like this. And they keep food warm for a long time. So, Emilia makes chips here – Pietro and Nina preparing the *patate*, the potatoes. Then, the chips are put in the metal tins to keep warm, into the *gelato* cart – no, the *patatine fritte* cart. Then you, Guto, the big man, haul the cart up the road to the park, where all the people are. Nina opens one of the tins. Oh! What a *delizioso*, *delizioso* delicious smell. Shout '*patatine fritte*' – you take a ha'penny a packet and offer the customer *sale e aceto* – salt and vinegar. Nina uses a big spoon to put the *patatine fritte* in a bag. You keep a penny for every ten bags you sell, what do you say to that?"

"A penny!"

"Yes. Each tin holds twenty bags of chips. We can fill six tins for the first go. What do you say?"

With a broad smile, Pietro holds out his hand to him.

Guto looks over at Nina. She's nodding and smiling.

"Yes," he says. "All right, Mister Bertorelli. What time?"

"Get down here by four. I've got you a white apron, see here?" He hands him a white apron from a hook behind the door. "And a cap on your head. You'll look like a *ragazzo patatine fritte* from Bardi! Oh, and now we are both working men, please call me 'Pietro', big man."

* * *

Reaching the Athletics Park means climbing one of the steep streets that cuts through the snaking terraces clinging to the valley sides.

The ice cream cart, with its double layer of wood and its load of chips, is pretty heavy.

After reaching the Park, Nina and Guto find a sheltered and convenient spot to park the cart. They keep an old, thick blanket across the top of the tins of chips while speaker after speaker address the crowd from atop a wagon.

Eventually, the master of ceremonies calls on the final speaker. "I call on Dai Jenkins to say a word."

"Tell it like it is, Dai Lend Me!"

"Friends, they're offering us a low price per ton. They know what they're doing. They are goading us. They want to see us striking, angry, and picketing the pits. While we're in this position, they're already arranging how they'll get blacklegs in and out of the mines. They say they're offering sufficient to those who are willing to work sufficiently hard. All shameless and barefaced lies! They're ready to stand by and see us starve and then go back to work on our knees. Every man, woman and child will suffer, and what is a man to do when he sees his children crying as they face an empty cooking pot? The children have a right to live. But we can't live in these terraces on pennies while they live in their hoity-toity grand houses with their millions. We want work, not the idleness of a strike. And we want a fair wage for our families, not the pittance we're bringing home at the moment. We all feel the same way, believe the same thing. Because we have all suffered in the same way as each other. The time has come for us to halt the suffering, the time has come for us to carry the day!"

Dai Lend Me's eyes are ablaze. He steps down from the wagon with his cloth cap askew over his left ear.

"Wise words, Dai," comments one man at the front of the crowd.

"Lend me a fag," Dai says, pausing to get a light for his cigarette from the man who had praised him.

The main speeches have finished. The leaders at the various pits go on to discuss tactics and how they will work together.

At the back of the crowd, Nina opens the first tin to let the smell of chips rise into the sharp night air. Guto sprinkles vinegar over them, and adds salt from a large pot.

"Chips! Ha'penny a bag!" he shouts.

"*Patatine fritte!*" Nina calls out.

One or two buy a packet, and the aroma of chips being spread among the crowd as they work their way back through it makes other people fancy chips too.

"*Dew, dew!* These are lovely!"

"Where did you get them, Walt?"

"Bertorelli's cart, over there."

Before long there is a queue of adults and children waiting for bags of chips.

"They're extra-tasty in the open air, aren't they?" says Guto as he hands out the bags and accepts the halfpennies. "Help yourself to salt and vinegar, and move up so I can serve the next people, please."

Nina fills the bags with speed and skill and lines them up in a neat row ready for Guto. Before long they are on the fourth tin and the crowd is waiting expectantly for more.

There isn't enough for the whole queue.

"You can get more in the cafe!" Guto shouts, when they've sold the last tin. "Down the hill and turn right. You'll get some from Pietro and Emilia."

He helps Nina close the tins and stow them back tidily in the bottom of the cart. He takes off his white cap and apron and tosses them in, on top of the tins. He turns to Nina. She does the same with her cap and apron, and smiles.

"Good work," says Guto.

"*Bene*," she says.

"Come on."

Guto grasps the handles of the cart, lifts them up and starts pushing until the wheels are turning by themselves. It's lighter, and the hill back down to Dunraven Street looks dangerously steep to tackle with the little cart. He decides to manoeuvre the cart round until it's behind him, so he can brake by using his legs to brace against the street. Nina sees what he's trying to do and comes to stand between the cart's handles. She steadies one, allowing Guto to grasp the other with two hands.

In this way they work their way down the hill, slowly and

carefully. The crowd has long dispersed by now and the night huddles around the terraces of the valley.

Nina starts singing. It is a beautiful and haunting song.

"*Canzone Mamma*," she says, between verses. She sings another verse.

"Your mother's song – it's *trist*," says Guto, using the Welsh word.

"Ah, *triste*!" Nina says.

"The same word!" says Guto. "The same feeling too ..."

Guto thinks about one of his own mother's sad songs.

Nostalgic songs or no, the pair pulling the cart have a certain lightness in their step.

Chapter 17

Pietro comes to sit at their table in the cafe.

After unloading and washing the cart out in the back yard, Guto has joined Alun and Dic Tic Toc inside the cafe for a hot chocolate.

"Up on the mountain Saturday afternoon?" Pietro asks.

"Well, Pietro, it's a bit late in the season for blackberrying!" Alun says.

"Yes, the winter's coming. The clock says ..." Dic Tic Toc starts.

"No, no, not blackberries ..."

"Looking for coal, is it?" Alun says. "Some of us go up to the old coal levels above Nant-gwyn. We'll have to reopen some of them so we can scavenge coal for our houses once we're on strike ..."

"No, not coal ... *Pugni!*" Pietro mimes a boxer squaring up, both his fists up to his face.

"Keep your voice down, Pietro!" whispers Alun, glancing over his shoulder at the rest of the cafe. "Past the old Nant-gwyn levels, over the ridge to the hollow at Pant Coedcae, under Trwyn y Ffynnon. Under the trees, five o'clock. Be careful who you let know."

"And Wil Wallop? Will he be ...? There's an eager smile on Pietro's face.

"Our Wil versus Ifor the Kid from Gilfach-goch."

"I've seen Ifor the Kid already," Pietro says. He has shoulders like two barrels. His right fist under his nose, but it is his left that is dangerous. He holds it out to the left, then whips it in like a snake ... His left hook, Wil needs to keep his eye out for that ..."

"You know your boxing, Pietro," Alun says.

"Ah! *Italiano* – fought hard to get work," Pietro says, shrugging his shoulders. "Lots of *Italiano* working on the railroads in America. Heavy work. Strong lads. But other men wanted the work. Complaining the *Italiano* are working for less pay for long hours. So ..."

Pietro starts to act fist fighting again.

"Yes, yes – but leave off with the fists now, Pietro, eh?"

"Now is not the time," says Dic Tic Toc.

"I didn't know Italians were boxers as well," Guto says. "I thought it was only Welsh miners that were boxers."

"Oh, no, no, no!" Pietro turns to hail his father, who is behind the counter.

"Hey! Papà!" He beckons him over to their table. "This is what he – Amadeo – did when he was in Paris. He's as hard as nails!"

Pietro explains to his father the gist of the conversation, that the lads didn't believe that there were any Italian stars in the boxing world.

"Francesco Conte," Amadeo declares.

"Who?" asks Alun.

"Frankie Conley," explains Pietro. Alun and Dic nod, obviously familiar with the name. He had become the bantamweight boxing champion of the world earlier in the year.

"You see," explains Pietro, "America does not like Italian names. So if a boxer wants to fight there, he changes his Italian name to something that sounds as if he is from Ireland. You've heard of T. C. O'Brien? Well, Antonio Caponi is his real name. And Fireman Jim Flynn? His name is Andrea Chiariglione. Boxing is the sport of poor people, and poor people have to change many things to please the money that runs things."

"That's more than likely why the Gilfach man is Ifor the Kid," says Alun.

"But Wil Wallop is a Welshman! Is he good? I've heard great things!" says Pietro.

"He's been fighting underground since he was twelve years old," Alun says. "When boys start work in the pits, there's a fight in the holes in the face every now and again, when we break to drink our cold tea. Boys of about the same weight. Two holes near each other in the floor of the tunnel and the boys in the holes, up to their waists. Fists then, until one submits. Oh, it's hard, believe me. Walloping – but you can't step back or fall: the holes are too narrow. The colliers lay bets. And Wil was the victor. He's got a really powerful right hand – he could floor a bullock."

"And on the mountain?" Pietro asks.

"This'll be the first time for Wil to be in a proper fight on the mountain. But if you're good in those holes, you're good anywhere. It teaches you to see in the dark. It teaches you to shift your head out of the way in a flash. It teaches you how to deal with a punch, how to take it but keep going and punch back. It's an education as a boxer – and an education as a collier too."

"Will there be bets on Saturday?" asks Pietro.

"Whoever wins between Wil and Ifor gets three shillings—"

"Three shillings!" Pietro turns to his father. "*Tre scellini!*"

"And the loser gets one shilling," says Alun.

"And there'll be bets?"

"There'll be bets among the crowd," Dic answers. "Ifor the Kid is the favourite, so the odds'll be good on Wil. So this time there's big money to be made."

"And big money to be lost, too," says Alun.

* * *

"Elevenpence, Mam," Guto says, opening his hand after arriving back at Number 17. "I bought tea for Alun and Dic to pay them back, but my own hot chocolate was from Pietro."

"Chip money. That'll come in handy for us," Beti says, walking over to the jug.

"No!" Guto says, glancing over at Eira, sitting in the fireside chair. "That's for Llew. You keep it to go towards the cost of the doctor."

"How was he this afternoon, Beti?" Alun asks.

"His temperature's better. The fever's losing its grip on him."

"Oh, good news. What the little one needs now is time." Alun turns his attention to Dewi, and tries to hold his hand as he staggers about, hands in the air. "And how's this little scamp doing, eh?"

He squats down and gives Dewi's chest a playful punch

with his fingers. Dewi quickly turns and gives his hand a punch to get it out of the way.

"Oh! This one's raising his fists as well. I hear that you, Moc, were a bit of a slugger in the ring in your time. This one's a chip off the old block too."

"Enough of that now," Moc says. "That was years and years ago."

"I should think so too," Beti says tersely.

Eira gets up from her chair and places her teacup on the kitchen table.

"Is that going to wash itself?" Beti asks. As she does so, she realises that something is missing from her daughter's hand. "And where's the ring? Mam's ring?"

"Um ...it's upstairs, under my pillow," Eira quickly replies, and walks out of the room.

* * *

Early on Saturday afternoon, his shift at the pit over, Moc is gathering together some old work tools in the shed in the far corner of the yard. Guto stands by the door, to receive them as Moc passes them out to him.

"Here we go ... sledgehammer ...old mandrel ... sacks ... saw ...spade ... axe ..."

"Why do we need an axe and a saw, Dad?"

"We might need to prop up the level if it goes in deep."

As bare-knuckle fighting is illegal, there is a danger that the police at the station on the main street will notice that something's afoot if a big crowd of people all make for the mountain at the same time. The plan, therefore, is to go early, do a bit of work looking for coal, and then go over towards Coedcae later.

Moc, Guto, Alun, Edward, Dicw and Wiliam walk up, up above Nant-gwyn. They climb over an old waste tip and down into a hollow where a small stream flows out from the base of the tip.

"Over that rise there," Moc says. "There's an old workings. We'll go and have a squint at what's there."

Under old thorn bushes and through bracken that now conceals some of the remains, Moc and Alun clear a path to the dark opening. Two wooden posts still support the wooden lintel that holds the roof in place.

Alun directs a kick at one of the posts and it collapses. The lintel falls, followed by a shower of small stones from the roof of the level.

"Right, Guto and I will look for timber and you clear this pile away," Alun says.

"Wil, you sit on this lump of wood," Moc says, flinging one of the old props into the shade and leaving the tin jack nearby. "Remember to drink enough water. You need to keep yourself fit."

Before long Alun finds a young ash tree beside the little stream. He starts to pound his axe into the trunk and Guto watches in wonder as the chips of wood fly out so easily. In no time at all, the ash tree is lying across the stream.

"You get to work with the saw now, Guto!" says Alun, wiping his forehead with the back of his hand. "Tidy the bottom end first, and then I'll measure two lengths from there."

Within the hour, two posts are in place at the entrance and the way is clear to walk further into the level. Moc has brought candles with him.

"Isn't there a danger of gas?" asks Dicw, when he sees the naked flame.

"No, we're not going far enough in, or deep enough into the rock," Moc replies. "These were just trial levels. They were searching for the main vein twenty years ago or more. That's well below the bed of the valley. But we could find a few small strands in the rocks up here. It wouldn't pay them to open a pit here, but it'll be good enough for us when we're on strike."

The tunnel is no more than ten yards long, running upwards. All of them spend a while examining the sides of the tunnel, a stretch each. After a quarter of an hour, Edward, Dicw's brother, calls Moc over.

"Look at the rock here, Moc. It runs level here, but down by my feet it runs on end. If we dig down through the bottom of the tunnel we could see how far down it runs. Maybe it's a little vein?"

"No harm in giving it a go, Ted," says Moc. "You've got a good eye, I'll say that for you." Dicw and Guto, fetch us that pickaxe here."

The lads set to with the pickaxe and, as the earth breaks up, Moc and Edward shovel it into their sacks. After they have filled five sacks and carried them out of the tunnel, Moc calls everyone over. He clears out the bottom of the hole, as well as the wall below the level of the tunnel floor, and then lowers his candle in and holds it against the rock face. They can see a gleam as the light is reflected.

"Mandrel!" calls Moc.

He aims two skilful blows at the bottom of the hole and the base of the wall and they hear rock loosening. Moc lifts the lumps out and holds the rock in the candlelight for the rest to see.

"Look at it, *bois*. The curse of this valley. The black treasure that enriches some men and kills others. I reckon this little vein is about five to eight inches thick here. So we can follow it for a while. We'll take out one sackful for each house today, isn't it, so we can say we've done something."

They were sitting on two sacks filled with coal and the waste wood, having a smoke and admiring the view, when Tal, the man with the scarred face, finds them. By now the hole in the floor of the tunnel has been refilled with loose stone to keep the treasure hidden for the future.

"Ready to give 'im an 'iding?" Tal asks sharply, as Wil stands up. "Come on, le's see those feet move."

Wil skips about to speed up his nimble footwork.

"Tha's it, keep goin'. Keep out of the way of tha' left 'and of 'is. It's a snake, remember. Left hook. Right, give the leaves on tha' tree over there a thrashin'. There you go, you've got a better reach in your arm than 'im. Keep that arm straight to keep him at bay. 'Ee likes comin' in low, like a bull – watch 'is 'ead. 'Ee thinks 'e's got a fist in his 'ead, the way he rams it forward first. No, 'old your right jab back ... Don't give it to 'im too early, or 'ee'll see it coming. You might as well send 'im a letter to tell 'im it's on its way ... Let 'im tire 'imself ... Poke 'im in the eyes ... 'ee won't see it comin' then ..."

Wil warms up for half an hour like this, then Tal calls a break.

"Tha's enough. Sack over your shoulders now, and another over your 'ead. Don' get cold. Plenty of water ... What time is it, Moc, mun?"

"Four."

"It's time for you all to go down. Get up the front, close to the rope, to support the lad. We'll go down when we need to be there."

Moc goes over to Wil, puts an arm round his shoulders, pulls his head towards his heart gives him a squeeze. He turns and walks across the slope in the direction of Coedcae, with the rest of them following behind.

*   *   *

As Eira makes to leave Number 17 that afternoon, Beti grabs her hand.

"Mam's ring is not upstairs, under your pillow. Where is it? I want it when this baby is born."

Eira pulls her hand away and looks at the floor.

"I haven't got it. I had to take it to Goodmans the Pawn to get money to pay the never-never."

"But it's been on my finger through every birth. Fetch it for me. My fingers have started to swell already, like my feet. I have to put it on now, or it'll be too late."

Chapter 18

There are about fifty men standing in the shelter of the trees in Coedcae by the time the Eleanor Street friends arrived. The supporters are standing separately.

"Those are the Gilfach lads over there, below that rock outcrop," Alun explains. "We'll keep clear of them, shall we?"

Although Alun had given him a mischievous wink, Guto can't help feeling uneasy and rather nervous. These are hard, scarred men up here, not young lads out for a bit of fun.

In the middle of the hollow, a rough and ready boxing ring has been erected. Four tree trunks from the surrounding trees, probably cut down that morning, support a thick rope suspended about four feet off the ground.

Moc walks over towards a group of miners from Pandy Colliery. Several of them come forward to wish him "best of luck for the lad". A stone's throw away, another little huddle nod their heads, acknowledging him.

"Llwynypia men," Alun explains. "There's some from Cwm Clydach as well. And Pen-y-graig. There's no saying who they're backing. Everyone wants to back the winner, of course. Wants to make a bob or two."

Just then, a short man comes into view. He is holding his cap in his hand as he smooths his other hand over his completely bald head. He carries a white cloth bag and is accompanied by a tall, dark, skinny man with his cap pulled down low over his eyes. Those eyes miss nothing as they dart from one person to another, thinks Guto.

"A penny for men, a ha'penny for butties *bach*," says the baldy, putting his cap back on. The money clinks into the bag. "Let's hope more than this turn up, or we won't have enough to pay the boxers!"

But he has no need to worry. Other groups arrive along the mountain paths from every direction.

"Look, there's Cabbage White and the Ely lot," says Edward, who, by now, knows the men from that pit. He walks over to them, and then returns suddenly.

"What's up with you, mun?" Moc asks. "You're like a woman getting the clothes off the line when it starts raining. Stand still, *y jiawl*!"

"I can't wait for things to start," Edward admits.

"Hadn't we better get ourselves closer to the ring?" Alun suggests.

"We'll go down to the far post, over there," Moc says. "The low sun won't be in our eyes then."

After they have crossed to their corner, Guto sees that Pietro and his father have arrived. The elderly Italian is grinning from ear to ear. He is clearly familiar with such occasions.

Guto gives them a wave, but on their way over to him, they pause to have a word with a man in a cloth cap This man looks different from the miners. He has a card with numbers on it in the top pocket of his jacket and papers in his hand. It's a very quick conversation. Amadeo and Pietro dip into their pockets, shake hands with the man in the hat. Each receives a piece of paper from him and walks on. The whole thing is over in seconds.

"*Buon giorno!*" says Pietro, and his father lifts his cap to greet them. "The bookie's giving tight odds. A shilling down, one shilling and sixpence back on Wil, and one shilling and threepence back on Ifor the Kid."

"We're holding off from placing our bets for the time being," Moc says. "We're waiting until the two contestants arrive."

By a quarter to five, the crowd has grown and there's a shout from the slope above them.

"Ifor's arrived!"

The fighter and his team come into view. He is wearing short trousers to the knee, white socks, and light, leather, calf-length boots, laced up with white laces. He has a white towel across his shoulders, but apart from that is naked from the waist up. He raises his fists in the air, acknowledging of the cheers of his supporters.

When he smiles, Guto notices that he doesn't have many teeth left. He doesn't smile for long. He rolls his shoulders and throws a few punches into thin air. As he turns left and right, the crowd can see the pattern of blue coal dust scars on his arms and back. His face is very clean and his red hair is heavily oiled and brushed back off his forehead. He walks closer to the ring, with the whole presence of his body pushing forward. He leads with his head, his arms and fists following closely behind.

Guto is aware that the Gilfach-goch supporters are crowding round the bookie to place their bets, now they've seen their hero arrive.

Then he sees Wil and Tal arriving through the trees. No cheer goes up to proclaim their presence. They go over to a corner post on the left-hand side, to Guto and the rest, facing Ifor the Kid's team across the ring.

Many are still going to the bookie, a few studying Wil carefully before they produce their money.

What do they see in his brother? Wil is eight or nine years younger than Ifor, certainly lighter, and his shoulders are less broad. He's not as scarred across his back but he carries a few recent injuries on his face. The eyes, thinks Guto – Wil has dark, serious eyes. He is looking down at the ground in front of him. Ifor has blue eyes, hard eyes. They dart around the crowd, as if inviting them to enjoy seeing him give his opponent a painful thrashing.

Guto sees another face he's seen recently – George, the blackleg who was at the pithead at the Ely Colliery during the unofficial strike in September. He's heading for the bookie, with a sarcastic smile on his face as he passes Wil.

"There's only a few minutes to go," Moc says. "We'll lay our bets now. The odds'll be better now, you'll see."

And they were, too. Two shillings for a shilling if Wil wins; ninepence for a shilling if Ifor does. How did his father know, thinks Guto. There must not be much support for Wil, once the crowd has compared the two. The shouting is sure to follow the betting.

He is right. After ducking under the rope to enter the ring,

Ifor goes straight to the centre with his arms up, punching the air. A huge roar goes up along the edge of the woods. He stands in his corner and Wil ducks under the rope. He doesn't go to the middle, merely stares fixedly at the ground in front of him. There are one or two shouts from the crowd.

"Go for it, Wil!"

"Give him what for, Wallop!"

"Give him hell, Wil!"

The little, bald man with the money bag now has a whistle in his mouth. With his left hand he raises a handkerchief. Simultaneously, he blows the whistle and brings the handkerchief down. Ifor the Kid rushes to the centre of the ring. The fight has begun.

There is no referee in the ring. There are no rounds and no breaks. There are no boxing gloves. This is a hard, mountain fight; a fight where the two of them will pummel each other until one is down and cannot get up.

Wil doesn't rush to the centre to engage with Ifor. He holds back and Ifor keeps coming forward, his head jutting out and his fists like two shields in front of his face.

He thinks he's cornered Wil at his corner post, but at the last second, Wil dances sideways on tiptoes before darting to the left. He has given half a suggestion to Ifor's left fist and, without hesitation, the more experienced fighter whips his famous fist towards him. But, by now, Wil is no longer in front of him, and Ifor is left hugging the post.

Ifor immediately goes for Wil. Wil moves backwards from post to post and Ifor throws punches. One at Wil's shoulder. One at his fist. One in his chest. But none of these do much damage. The crowd grows more vocal with every blow that makes contact.

Wil keeps away from the open ground in the centre of the ring, keeping Ifor circling round the perimeter. From corner to corner they move, with Ifor still attacking, still punching forward like a bull, but with Wil managing to keep out of trouble.

But after a minute or so of this, Ifor takes a quick step to the centre of the ring instead of following Wil to the next post. The pair stand, regarding each other. Wil has his back to the post. Ifor takes a tiny step towards him, lessening the gap – left and right – through which Wil could escape. Ifor takes another step towards him – he's in control of the situation now. He shoots out his fists left and right, signalling that there's no escape for Wil in either direction. He's cornered and Ifor is coming for him.

Before he can be trapped against the post and the rope, Wil steps smartly forward and straightens his left arm, shooting his left fist at his opponent's forehead, hitting him right on the eyebrow. He draws that fist back after landing his right fist on Ifor's cheek. The seasoned scrapper raises his fists high and the next two punches from Wil land on those fists without injuring his adversary.

Ifor steps forward and Wil's trunk is exposed now. He pummels Wil's ribs hard. Two, four blows each side. Those do damage. The ribs tighten and Wil cannot keep his fists up to protect his face. Bam! Ifor's right fist lands on Wil's nose and tears fly from his eyes.

"Watch the left!" Tal shouts. Just as well he did. Wil

inclines his head to the left as Ifor whips out towards him.

The fist glances off the side of Wil's head. But Wil sees a way out. He positions his feet as if his body is going to follow his head, then slides like an eel past Ifor's right fist, which meets nothing but air and he flails like a windmill.

The contender from Gilfach-goch is slower this time in his pursuit of Wil round the ropes. Guto notices that one of his eyebrows is bloody and that the other eye is turning black. But his brother's nose is bleeding too.

All of a sudden, Wil changes his tactic. He steps into the centre of the ring. He's still moving in a circle, but a much smaller one. Ifor follows him, hitting him with both fists when he's close in. They are hard blows. Guto can hear every smack echoing round the hollow and he hears his brother's heavy groan. Why has he gone into the middle?

A right-hand fist lands on Wil's lip. He shakes his head to clear his eyes. He didn't see it coming. Then an upper cut catches him under his jaw, lifting him an inch or two into the air. He staggers backwards until he's on the rope. He spits, and Guto sees something white shoot out of his mouth. His brother has lost a tooth.

The Gilfach bullock goes for him, his head pushing forward and his body following. Wil raises his fists to hide his face. He gets thumped time after time in the ribs and stomach. It goes on and on.

"Remember 'ow you fought in them 'oles, Wil!" Tal is trying to urge him on.

Suddenly something clicks in Wil's brain. Hitting and being hit was what happened in the holes down in the mine.

Wil knows he's learned to endure pain. Ifor continues battering him, but now Wil is hitting back.

He stands up so that his back isn't against the rope. He keeps his back straight. He throws every punch with the full reach of his arm and this puts more weight behind every blow. Yes, he's still being punched himself, but now his punches are leaving their mark on Ifor. Wil aims for his face. Especially the eyes. Ifor's left eye is very black and is starting to close. Blood is pouring into his right eye.

Wil gets in another blow to the left eye. The crowd is going wild by now. This is what they want to see – two men unremittingly slugging it out. Wil gets two more fists in his ribs but he lands his left fist on the wound that is already flooding Ifor's right eye. Ifor takes a step back into the centre of the ring. Wil escapes leftwards.

Ifor searches for him, but by the time he's turned, Wil is back in the middle and he lands his left fist in the middle of Ifor's face. This time it's Ifor's turn to groan as he hears the crowd.

"Come on, Ifor! Finish him off!" someone yells.

"Beat him to the ground, mate!"

It's Wil who holds himself squared up now. Head up and long arms out in front of him, he deals with the blows Ifor is raining on him. Then, Ifor suddenly rushes him and pushes him back with both fists. There's power behind the attack and Wil is back on the rope once more. Ifor goes in, past Wil's long arms, his fists in Wil's ribs. And then Guto sees Ifor draw his head back and plant his forehead on the bridge of his brother's nose.

"That was a headbutt!" Guto protests.

"There's no rules here, *bachan*," Alun says.

Guto sees his father form a fist with one hand and hit the palm of the other with it.

Wil's nose is smashed. It's flattened and bloody and bent. He's having trouble breathing because there is so much blood spurting through his nostrils. He manages to go to the left once more, but Ifor is ready for him. He stamps on his boot and grinds his foot into the earth. It is as if Wil has been nailed in place, helpless. He can do nothing to avoid the heavy blows facing him.

By now neither can see clearly. One of Ifor's eyes has been closed by the swelling and the other has blood running into it, while Wil's broken nose is affecting his vision. He's transported back once again to the hole down the mine. There's nothing for it but to lash out with his fists in the hope that one or two hit the mark.

"The whip ... watch out for the whip!" warns Tal again.

Wil can't see him, but he hears the shout. He moves his head back and levels out his right fist with all his strength as Ifor's body follows his left hook. Wil's fist sinks into Ifor's midriff and he doubles over, winded. Guto hears the air exploding out of the Gilfach man. Wil's foot is released. He moves to the right and shoots his left fist into Ifor's face. Ifor wobbles backwards and that's when Wil releases his right fist. It comes from somewhere deep down, with the miner's full strength behind it. Ifor's arms dart out sideways, and Wil catches him neatly under his chin. He tips backwards as if shot. He lands on his back on the grass, his arms spread wide.

The small, bald man blows his whistle.

Moc, Alun and Pietro squeeze their way through the throng to grab the bookie's jacket to make sure they get their winnings. Guto hurries over to Wil, who is bending down under the rope to have a word with baldy.

Then there is a shout from the edge of the wood.

"Police! Police! Scarper!"

Guto hears the sound of police whistles approaching quickly up the path.

Chapter 19

As the men of Number 17 bid good evening to the Mainwarings on Eleanor Street, their pockets and their hearts are full. But their joy doesn't last for long.

They have successfully evaded the police. Once Moc and the other men had claimed their winnings, they went down to Wil beside the ring. The little, bald man is not at all happy, and neither is the tall, dark one but despite this the three shillings are safely transferred from the white bag to Wil's hands.

"Get out of here!" Alun says. "Guto's got your shirt – put it on, Wil. And your cap, and pull it down over that black eye. We'll go back round the mountain to the old coal level."

"Good idea," agrees Moc. "The police will be expecting men to go down the mountain. We'll go in the other direction and wait for a while for things to calm down. Come on, Wil, so we can wash your face in the stream on the way over."

An hour later, with coal dust from the sacks on their faces – the dust helping to hide Wil's bruises – they come down the mountain path to the highest terraces of houses.

"No, we've been looking for lumps of coal in the old tips, we have," is their ready answer to the policeman stationed at the mountain gate. No, they hadn't heard anything about any boxing.

But when Moc opens the front door of his home, he sees at once that something is amiss. Dewi is sitting at the top of the stairs.

"Dewi! What are you doing at the top of the stairs? Guto, go and fetch him in case he falls. Why isn't Beti watching him? Beti! Where is the woman?"

He pushes the kitchen door open. In the middle of the floor, the bathtub is on its side. A bucketful of water has been spilled across the whole floor, and the empty bucket has rolled towards the fireplace. Between the bathtub and the table, Beti's body is sprawled. She is motionless.

"Beti!" Moc cries, rushing over to her.

"Careful, Moc," Alun says, dropping his sack of coal to the floor. "It could be dangerous to move her."

"Blood!" says Wil. "She's been bleeding ..."

The blood is colouring the water on the floor around Beti's skirt.

Guto arrives, with Dewi in his arms.

"Give him here," Alun says. "Go and fetch Gwyneth Out the Way. Quick!"

Gwyneth lives in Trinity Road, next to the Catholic Church and School. Down the street and up the hill. Guto is so out of breath he can only gasp out his request to the midwife. But she's taken care of every birth in these terraces for twenty years or more, and although she only grasps "Mam" ... "floor" ... "blood", she immediately understands the situation. She grabs her bag and gallops off up the street. Guto can barely keep up with her.

"Out the way," she says to the men who are dejectedly bent over Beti. "Why don't you do something useful?"

She looks from one to the other.

"A bowl of hot water! Clean towels! Open that window over there so we can have a bit of fresh air."

Her fingers encircle Beti's wrist and she takes out her watch. Guto can see she's counting. Looking at the short, round woman, he can see that she's a safe pair of hands. She has muscled arms, like a boxer's, and a square and determined face. Everything about her says that she won't put up with any nonsense.

"Her blood pressure is low. Dangerously low. That's why she's passed out ... Who carried this bathtub into the kitchen?"

Her eyes blaze as her gaze scans the two men and the two lads. All four look down at their boots.

"Don't tell me that you've been letting her do the heavy work in the house in her condition! Are you mad? You know how long a shift underground is?"

"Eight hours these days," Alun says.

"Yes, you miners have battled to reduce your hours. But women work twice that."

"But ..." Moc starts to say.

"'But she only does housework' – that's what you're going to say, isn't it?"

Gwyneth looks at him like a lioness. "I'll get back to you on that one, *gw'boi*. But for now, help me to turn her over and get her straight. You two – bring the towels and bowl upstairs. What's your name?"

"Alun."

"Oh, the lodger, is it? Always wanting something, I'll bet. Get hold of her under her armpits and lift her carefully when

I say so. Moc – get a hold under the back of her knees. Ready ...? Right, lift her. Out the way – I'm going upstairs ahead of you to get the bed ready."

While the men get Beti up to the bedroom, Gwyneth opens the window and pulls back the bedclothes. Over the bottom sheet she lays two clean towels.

"What the hell have you done to your face?" she asks Wil, as she takes the basin of hot water from him. "And don't tell me you walked into a post underground. I recognise fighting-on-the-mountain injuries when I see them. Go downstairs and wash that sorry face of yours and I'll take a look at that flat nose after."

Alun and Moc have reached the door, and Beti's face is still as white as the sheets on the bed.

"Onto the bed. Careful! She needs another pillow under her head."

Guto hurries to fetch the pillow from Eira's bed.

"Out the way! Go and make a cup of strong, sweet tea for her, you two. You know where the teapot and the tea are kept, hopefully?"

Alun and Moc nod like pet lambs and retreat downstairs.

"When did your mother last have a square meal?" Gwyneth asks Guto.

"She had breakfast this morning, and she must have had dinner."

"Did you see her eat dinner?"

"No, we weren't here."

"And what about breakfast?"

"She'd had something before we got up, she said."

"And supper last night?"

"She'd have something in the kitchen while she was clearing the dishes, she said."

"Another house of fools! Rhondda's full of them. The women starve themselves so the men can have the food to have the strength to work in the pits. And no one seems to think that the women need strength! Look at this arm. It's as thin as a hazel twig. She needs nourishment too, you hear."

Guto feels his eyes filling up. This woman has walked into the house and shown them things they've never seen or noticed before.

"There's no time to be crying, *crwt*!" Gwyneth says. "Go to the shop and ask for a tin of black treacle. Are there any eggs in the house?"

"No, Wil had the last egg this morning ..."

"He needed strength while his mother was so frail, is it? Go and get half a dozen eggs and a pint of milk too."

Guto shoots down the stairs and out through the front door like a whirlwind. There is no time to fetch money from the jug. He could add the items to their slate at Wilkins' shop, and if the other shoppers looked down on him, well stuff them!

When Moc goes back upstairs, his tread is soft and light. He taps on the bedroom door before entering.

"Gwyneth ... is ... is ... she alright, Gwyneth?"

"Alright? Are you out of your mind, man? She's as weak as a kitten and has lost a lot of blood. I expect it's her who's been carrying coal in for the fire? And filling the boiler? And heaving the bathtub in and out? And washing work clothes?

And drying them? And pegging them out on the line? And running out to fetch them back in when it rains? And blackleadding the range? And cleaning the house from top to bottom? And baking and cooking and shopping and scrubbing and ironing and polishing, and nursing and minding the little one, and making everything nice? And carrying a baby in her womb for over eight months on top of that?"

Moc's head hangs lower with every question, and he seems to retreat into himself.

"And the place was so spick and span that you had no idea that she'd worked at all! Well, I want it spick and span. Get yourself and those other two lummocks into the kitchen. Mop the floor, dust, polish the table and the cupboards, blacklead the range – and I want to see the place sparkle! And the back kitchen, and out the back! And I want to see a good fire and a full boiler ... and then you can make some leek *cawl* for supper."

"But ..."

"Out the way. Oh, and—"

"Yes?"

"There's a girl lives her too, isn't there?"

"Yes. Eira."

"Well fetch her."

"But she works in Elias Davies' shop ..."

"Well, you can tell that one to whistle – I want her here. Now."

Guto runs in through the front door as his father is running out into the street.

"What next?" Guto asks, showing his purchases to Gwyneth.

"I want you to warm the black treacle on the hob of the range. Loosen the lid on the treacle tin first, or it'll explode. And warm up some milk. Put two eggs in bowl and beat them with a fork. With a teaspoon, give the treacle a stir every so often until it's runny and has warmed through. Then put a little of the warm milk in with the eggs and add three teaspoonfuls of black treacle. Mix it all in with the spoon and bring it up here. Eggs and treacle – the best thing for someone who's starved themselves."

In the kitchen, no one says a word. The work is so alien to every one of them, they have to concentrate. Wil's injuries in the ring are forgotten. He's more afraid now of not doing the housework properly.

When Moc returns with Eira in tow, she goes straight upstairs to the bedroom.

"So you're the 'Milady' of this house, are you?" Gwyneth lays into her in a no-nonsense fashion. "Well, I brought you into the world, *grotan*. It was a February and the whole valley was in the grip of winter. I'll tell you straight, my girl, your mother won't see another winter unless we sort out everything she needs in the next few hours."

"Oh!" says Eira, as the seriousness of the situation sinks in.

"Come here and help me undress her and wash her and get her into her nightdress to start with."

"But I don't—"

"It's time to do as you're told, *grotan*, not think up excuses. Lift her into a sitting position from that side. And do it NOW!"

When Guto brings the bowl into the bedroom, Gwyneth

sets Eira to work easing the concoction, a spoonful at a time, from the bowl to her mother's lips. Instinctively, her lips accept it and she swallows.

"Keep at it, *grotan*. I'm going down to have a word with your father."

When Gwyneth opens the kitchen door, the men all jump back from her, each looking guiltily at their handiwork.

"Pass me the jug," she says to Moc.

He obeys instantly but doesn't meet her eye.

"There's nothing in it at the moment ..."

"What sort of men live in this house, for goodness' sake?"

"But we've got money to put in the jug tonight!" He remembers about his winnings on the mountain. He puts his hand in his pockets. "Look – six shillings in this pocket, another six in this one ..."

"And I've got three shillings," Wil says. The money is piled up on the table in front of Gwyneth.

"And I've another ten shillings," Alun says.

"And I'll have another threepence the next time I take the chip cart out," Guto says, trying to please her.

"It's a start," Gwyneth says. "Rhondda – the richest place in the world for coal and the place of the poorest women in the world. It doesn't make sense, does it? We have to call in the doctor, Moc. Yes, it's going to cost. But if we don't it'll cost the life of your wife and the little baby she's carrying. She's lost blood and she's still not properly conscious. We have to get her back. That's the first step. Moc, go and fetch the doc."

Moc puts his cap on and heads out into the street without a second's hesitation.

"Right, *blodyn*," she says to Wil. "Sit down in that chair by the table for me to get a look at that nose. Head back."

She carefully feels the nose, with Wil gripping the edge of the table in pain.

"I'll have to straighten this before it swells any further, or there'll be no room to move it later." She turns to Alun. "Oxman, go and fetch a handkerchief to mop the blood."

With a handkerchief tied under Wil's chin, Gwyneth gets hold of the nose between her finger and thumb and gives it a tug and a half turn. They hear a click as the bones move pack to their proper position, followed by Wil's scream.

"Don't be such a baby! No, on second thoughts, a baby can withstand more pain than that. Did you know that every bone in a baby's head shifts as it's being born. *Dew, dew* – it's a shame that men aren't as tough as they were when they were babies! Right, I'm going to pack some cotton into both your nostrils. You'll have to breathe through your mouth for a while. Make sure you turn them every hour, to keep the holes open or you'll be speaking with a nasal whine for the rest of your life. Take them out before you go to bed and you should be fine."

Before going out through the door and back upstairs, she turns back.

"When are you planning on starting to clean? And I don't smell any sign of supper coming from the fire over their either."

Chapter 20

"I've brought seven children into the world in this room. How many of them have lived?" Gwyneth asks Eira, when she is back upstairs.

"Five of us. But Llew is in the Tyntyla Sanatorium at the moment."

"Five still living out of seven. That's good going. It's no surprise that the jug is empty. Half of those born in the Rhondda die before they've out of childhood. This is the worst place in the whole of Britain to give birth. I'll tell you this, Great Britain isn't much help to you if you're a child of this valley."

"It's worse here than anywhere else?" Eira says, surprised. "But how is can that be?"

"Look at the houses here to start with. The place is so small and so many live here. The houses have been thrown together quickly and poorly, they're damp and there's no fresh air. The terraces are on top of each other. The front step of one street is virtually on the roof of the privy of the terrace below!"

Eira looks at her as if seeing the valley as it really is for the first time.

"And don't even get me started on the privies. Yes, they're plumbed-in these days and the sewage goes somewhere, but because the ground is full of holes under the works, there are landslips and the weight is on the pipes. They burst and the filth goes into every little ditch, stream and river. The water's not fit to drink here. It's a paradise for rats and all the worst human diseases."

"But people are still flocking here to live."

"And what sort of living is it? A whole family living in a cellar with damp from the earth creeping through the walls and into their lungs. These houses are more dangerous than the pits."

"It's the men that get the worst of it," Eira insists. "There's not a week goes by without one of them that lives in these streets getting seriously injured at work."

"True, and there's over fifty of them a year killed in the pits of Rhondda. One a week! But I've seen the reality of the women – there's more housewives than colliers die young in this valley."

"But being a miner is heavy work."

"It's heavy work carrying a baby and giving birth to it, and doing everything else in the house as well."

Eira turns to look at her mother.

"She's ... she's ... Mam's going to be alright, isn't she?" The silence that follows is long and awkward.

"She's not going to die, is she?" Eira asks.

Gwyneth goes to the window impatiently.

"Where is that doctor? Men!" She turns back suddenly to Eira. "You said that one of the little ones is in the San?"

"Llew."

"How old is he, and how is he?"

"Three. Diphtheria. He's had a very high temperature. His

throat has swelled up and a white growth is covering it and starting to block his windpipe."

"That's another curse of this valley. It all stems from one bad source."

"What do you mean?"

"Poverty. Who looks after the jug in the kitchen?"

"Mam."

"Who knows how much money is in there? Keeps enough back to pay the rent, so you're not turned out into the street? Who decides how much to spend on what goes into the *cawl*? And who lets her own clothes wear thin and full of holes so her husband and children can be dressed decently?"

Eira shakes her head to try and hold back her tears.

"And who keeps the body and soul of the household together, draws you all together as a family when it's so much easier for you to go your separate, selfish ways?"

Eira stuffs her fist in her mouth.

As she does so, they hear a knock on the front dor.

Eira turns thankfully towards the stairs, and goes down to let the doctor in.

"Up the stairs and it's the door on the right. She's with Gwyneth Out the—"

"Gwyneth Out the Way?"

"Yes. She's with Mam."

The doctor smooths down his hair and brushes off his clothes and hands. Then he climbs the stairs, two at a time.

Eira is about to close the front door, but has second thoughts. She turns and runs upstairs to the bedroom she shares with the boys. She gropes about under her bed. She pulls out a pair of new shoes. Clutching them in her left hand she hurries back downstairs. She closes the front door behind her and walks towards Dunraven Street.

* * *

"How on earth do you make leek *cawl*?" Moc asks. "Put a mandrel or a crowbar in my hands and I'll know what to do with it. But if you give me a wooden spoon, I haven't got a clue."

"Well, I guess we need to chuck a bit of leek in, don't you think?" suggests Alun.

"Where will we get some? Does Cabbage White grow leeks now?" Moc asks.

"Yes," Guto replies. "But they're only small. They're not ready yet. I've seen some in the Co-op ... when was it? What about Wilkins?"

"You can forget that idea right now," Alun says. "I'll go down to the Co-op. I'm not in his pocket or paying rent to him. Do you want anything else while I'm at it?"

"What else goes into *cawl*, then?" Moc asks. "Spuds, maybe? Yes, I'd think so. Are there any in the back kitchen, Wil?"

While Wil is digging about in the back, Guto has a flash of inspiration.

"I saw Mam boiling up a big bone in the stew pot once," he says. "I think she said she was making *cawl*,"

"There we go, ask for a bone in the Co-op too, Alun."

"And what about a bit of parsley? I remember going to fetch some from the allotments."

"To late in the year for parsley," Alun says.

"I'm pretty sure they've got things growing in pots on the inside kitchen window sills in Bertorelli's," Guto suddenly remembers.

"Well, you go and ask if you can have some while I go to the Co-op," Alun says.

"I've found three big potatoes," Wil declares triumphantly, holding them up as if they are made of pure gold.

"Right, we'll have a knife each so we can peel and clean them," Moc says. "Best put some water on to boil in the pot first."

Moc takes a little knife out of the drawer. He sits at the table, holding the potato in his left hand to stop it rolling away. He tries to trim away the skin with the sharp knife in his right hand. Then he gives the potato a quarter turn with his left hand and carves the skin away again. Before long it looks more like a brick than a potato. The fingers of his left hand are all over the place, and then the inevitable happens.

"Hell's bells!" Moc has sliced off the top of one finger. With blood soaking into the potatoes, they look even more like bricks than before.

* * *

It is Nina who answers Guto's knock at the back door of the cafe this time. He's greeted with a warm smile. She indicates for him to follow her into the kitchen.

"*Buona sera, prego entra! Papà!*" Pietro appears.

"Ah! One of the *pugilatore*. The brave man with his fists of iron. Oh, Guto, it was a fight and a half!"

"You didn't have any trouble with the cops, did you?"

"*Polizia*? Ah! No, no. We were taking the old man, Papà, for a walk on a Saturday afternoon to get a bit of fresh air, of course! But ..." He puts his hand in his pocket and jingles the contents. "A good afternoon of work on the mountain, eh? But tell me – how is Wil? Is he alright ...?"

Pietro takes hold of his nose and wiggles it one way and then the other.

"Wil's nose is sort of alright now. Um ...it's Mam who's not alright."

"Not alright?" Pietro's face changes to one of concern. "The *bebè* ...? Is it on the way? Are they in difficulty? O, *Mamma mia.*"

A rush of Italian pours from his mouth as he turns to Emilia and Nina.

"She's fallen in the kitchen," Guto explains. "She's in bed now, but she's not coming round."

"Ah! *No-no. La caduta!*" Pietro cries.

"And she's lost blood ..."

"*Ooo! Ematica! No-no-no!*" Pietro's eyes are wide and he has visibly paled.

Emilia steps into the middle of the floor.

"*Nina – Il timo,*" she says, handing her the scissors.

Nina lifts a pot of herbs off the window sill and cuts a generous bunch with the scissors.

"Parsley?" Guto asks.

"*No, no,*" says Emilia. "*Il timo.*"

"It is thyme," Pietro explains, getting a grip on himself

once more. "Its leaves will revive the body. It purifies the blood and is good for the belly. Chop it up fine and put it in ..."

"In leek soup?" suggested Guto.

"*Bene, bene!* Leeks from Wales, thyme from Italy, there's nothing better," says the Italian.

When Eira returns home, she goes straight upstairs to the bedroom. There's a strong aroma of smelling salts and other strong chemicals. The doctor is holding her mother's arm and injecting something into the vein. Gwyneth is busy pinching Beti's cheeks and is holding a bottle under her nose. She's been lifted up to a sitting position again, with only a sheet over her. Eira can see that her legs are open wide on the bed.

"She's starting to come round," Gwyneth is saying. "We can't lose her now. Come over here, Eira, beside the bed and talk to her. A familiar voice can work miracles at a moment like this."

"What is the doctor giving her?" Eira asks, as she moves over to do what Gwyneth has told her to.

"Oh, something expensive. Something to strengthen the muscles or something, he said. She has to give birth to the baby ..."

"But it's not due for another fortnight or so, isn't it?"

"There's not one baby in the Rhondda stays in its mother's womb full term, *grotan*," Gwyneth says. "The mothers work too hard for that. Now talk to her."

"Mam? ... Mam?" Eira says hesitantly. Then, in a stronger voice, she says, "Mam, look what I've got here. Mam-gu's ring!"

Eira uncurls her fingers and holds the ring in the palm of her hand in front of her mother's face.

"It was missing, d'you remember? Well, I've got it back. And I'm going to put it on your finger now, exactly how you wanted it. No, it won't fit on the middle finger – that one's too swollen. And the two others too. But look – it fits snugly on the little finger. There we are, Mam. Your own mother's ring on your finger. It'll warm your blood, won't it? That's what you always told us, I remember now. You could feel the warmth of Mam-gu warming your own blood when you wear this ring ..."

Just then, Beti opens her eyes. Bloodshot, dazed eyes. She looks fearfully round the room.

"Wha ... what's going on here? What's happened to me ...?"

"Good lass," Gwyneth says to Eira, patting her arm. "Your voice did the trick."

"Maybe the medicine I gave her earlier is starting to work now," the doctor says.

"Pah! Chemists' concoctions! Since when have things like that understood people?"

The doctor stows his syringe back in his case and extracts his stethoscope.

"It should start working in an hour or two ..."

"I'll stay with her now," Gwyneth says.

"It's important to get the baby out promptly. She's too weak to push much. There's a great danger to the baby and to her ..."

The doctor pulls down the sheet, pushes up Beti's nightdress, and puts the horn of the stethoscope on her swollen belly and listens. He moves it about, still listening. The he puts it away in his case.

"As soon as possible," he says from the bedroom doorway. "And take good care of her before and after."

He goes down the stairs and out.

"What did he hear with that horn thing on Mam's belly now?" Eira asks.

"Out the way. I'll take over now. You get ready to hold her and bend her legs when I say. And here we go again, Beti. Can you hear me?"

Beti turns to face the voice at her bedside. Her cheeks are the same colour as the sheet, thinks Eira.

Chapter 21

"*Jiawch, bois*, that's good! A touch more salt, maybe." Alun tosses another pinch of salt into the *cawl*, which by now is bubbling over the fire. "I've worked up a good appetite slaving over this hot fire too. Could we have supper now, d'you think?"

"It'll be better for leaving it over the fire for a while to bring out the flavour," Moc says. "Wait and see how things are upstairs, isn't it?"

"Can we take things up to Mam now, d'you think?" Guto asks. "She'll get better quicker if she gets this thyme, Pietro said."

"No, she won't want it now. All in good time," Moc says. "But maybe Dewi'll have some. Do you want your supper, Dewi?"

Dewi walks towards him confidently and raises his hands to be lifted up to see what's in the pot.

"Can you see what it is? Lovely, isn't it?"

"I'll get a bowlful for him," Wil says. He ladles some soup into a bowl. "Come to the table, Dewi. It's hot, mind – but I'll blow on it for you."

"Wouldn't Llew be pleased to have some of it?" suggests Guto.

"I'll go with you," Alun says. "Come on, we'll put some in a jam jar, put a lid on it and we'll see how he is. Your mother won't be going for a while – one or other of us should go every day."

There's not much happening on the main street, even though it's Saturday night. Nobody much shopping, no one gathering at the theatre entrances.

"With the strike starting Tuesday, everyone's watching the pennies," Alun says.

"Will everyone be on strike this time?" Guto asks.

"Mabon hasn't succeeded in get better terms than two shillings and threepence a ton. We can't live in these valleys on so little. The miners who work for the Naval collieries at the Ely, Nant-gwyn and the Pandy have been locked out already. The rest, the Cambrian Company miners in Gilfach, Cwm Clydach and Llwynypia are walking out on the first of November – Tuesday. Then you'll have eleven thousand miners on strike. And there's talk that pits in the other valleys will stop production too. If the owners can unite to try and defeat the strikers, the workers can do exactly the same thing."

They go under the railway bridge and up towards Llwynypia. Dozens of policemen are standing at the entrance to the Glamorgan mine. They are wearing their black overcoats and hard, spiked helmets.

"*Jiw-jiw*, the police have arrived already, have they?" Alun remarks.

"I don't think they're all policemen from Tonypandy and Llwynypia, are they?" Guto asks.

"No, they pull them in from places like Cardiff and Swansea."

"Where are they staying?"

"You see the lights in those sheds at the pithead? I reckon they're using them as barracks for them."

"But there's no trouble here."

"No ... not yet."

"So the police have picked which side they're on already?" Guto ventures. "Whatever happens, they'll be against the miners?"

"That's how it's always been. And maybe that's how it'll always be. The wealth lies with the owners, and so does the vote, and so they've got the power over everyone in this area – and those clowns in the government in London too."

"They've got big feet, haven't they," Guto observes.

"And big truncheons too," says Alun.

They go on to the hospital. Guto holds his breath as he walks in through the doors. The mixture of smells makes him feel unsettled – the medical smells and disinfectant, but also the reek of patients and putrefaction. Alun tells one of the nurses who they are here to see.

"You'll both have to wear masks. Come with me."

She secures a white mask across the nose and mouth of each of them, with straps.

"The white growth is spreading and his mouth is foul," explains the nurse. "This is a disease that spreads person to person extremely easily. The bacteria are carried through the air from the patient to the next person – so the mask will protect you. But don't go too close to him either."

"Can't I give him a cwtsh?" Guto asks.

"No."

"But I share a bed with him at home. It's me that kept

him warm when he was cold in the night."

"You've been sharing a bed with him?" the nurse says anxiously.

"Yes, that's how it is in our house. There's not enough beds."

"It's like that all over the valley. Let's take a look at you."

The nurse squeezes Guto's throat with her finger and thumb and then she does the same to the glands under his chin. She feels the glands behind his ears.

"Let me take your mask off for a minute, and come over here into the light. Stick your tongue out. Say 'ahh!' for me."

She examines inside Guto's mouth. Then she nods and gently closes it. She produces a thermometer and takes his temperature.

"No, there's no sign that you've caught anything. And you don't have a temperature. Is everyone else at home alright?"

"Well, Mam's in the middle of giving birth to a new baby ..."

"*Dew, dew*, not another one in this valley!" says the nurse, as she re-ties Guto's mask. "Where are we going to put them all? And how many more beds will be needed in this hospital? Come on, follow me."

As they approach the bed, Guto and Alun can see clearly that Llew's neck is hugely swollen. This is no ordinary sore throat.

"How are you, Llew?" asks Guto from a distance.

His brother coughs harshly and painfully and groans.

"He's short of breath and that gives him a headache," the nurse says. "His windpipe is slowly closing and he's having trouble breathing and then he has this awful cough. The back of his throat, inside, is completely white now ..."

By pinching his nose and easing his jaw down, the nurse opens Llew's mouth and shines her torch in.

"Don't get too close to his breath!"

From afar Guto can see a thick blanket of white, like a solid coating of ice around the back of Llew's throat. He's never seen anything like it in his life.

"Isn't there any way of scraping that white stuff out of there?" he says.

"It's flesh that's rotted," explains the nurse. It'll either get better itself or more flesh will rot ..."

"And his throat will close up completely?"

"It's a cruel disease," the nurse says quietly.

"His mother's been painting that white coating with his wee," Alun says. "She can't be here tonight. So I'll—"

"That's an old wives' tale," the nurse says, almost inaudibly.

"Mam-gu said so. She did it and she knew what she was doing."

"The bottle and the little brush are in the cupboard the other side of the bed," says the nurse, turning to go. She points at Guto. "But he's not to touch the bottle or the brush or come any closer. This disease affects children far worse than adults."

Alun's task is awkward and laborious. It aggravates Llew and he gags between fits of coughing, although he has nothing to bring up.

"He sounds like a dog barking," Guto says, the deep furrows in his forehead reflecting the feelings in his heart.

The pair are subdued on the way home.

There are still crowds of policemen at the entrances to the Glamorgan Colliery at Llwynypia.

"Llwynypia's a much bigger pit than the Pandy, isn't it?" Guto says.

"Oh, yes. There's over three thousand four hundred workers here."

"They'll want a fair few coppers more here, won't they?"

"Let's see how it goes. The big powerhouse that produces electricity is here in Llwynypia. They use the electricity to pump five thousand gallons of water a minute out of the mine – if the electricity is cut, the pit will flood and more than likely will never reopen. The owners are bound to want to bring blacklegs in to work the pumps and furnaces in the powerhouse, and so they're expecting trouble here."

"The people in this valley don't have much to say to the blacklegs, do they?"

* * *

In the kitchen, Moc and Wil can hear the screams from the bedroom. Moc puts his hands over Dewi's ears when they're at their worst.

"Dear God, how much longer is this going on for!" he sighs.

Alun and Guto walk in and report on Llew's condition.

"Beti hovering between life and death upstairs, Llew hovering in the Sanatorium," Moc says, his head in his hands.

It's a long night. Dewi sleeps on his father's knee. None of them leave the kitchen to go to their own beds. Moc is sprawled in the fireside chair with his arms wrapped round Dewi when Eira comes down in the small hours. She crouches down next to his shoulder.

"Mam's asking for you, Dad," she whispers softly. "Gwyneth says you can go to her now."

"Is she ... she's not ...?" The questions stumble over each other in Moc's head.

"We've lost the baby, Dad. There was nothing we could do. It had died in the womb hours ago, Gwyneth said. Probably the loss of blood."

"But she ... Beti is ..."

"Go up and see her, Dad. I'll fetch a cup of tea up just now."

The bedroom door is ajar. When Moc pushes it open he notices his hand is shaking. As he walks into the room, Gwyneth is busy with a basin of water and the towels. Moc goes straight to the bed.

Beti opens her eyes.

"Moc ..."

Moc takes her hand.

"He didn't live, Beti?"

"It was a girl, Moc."

"Poor little thing! Oh! ..."

"I'm sorry, Moc."

"Shush now, my dear. It's not your fault ... How are you feeling now?"

Beti closes her eyes, her pain obvious.

"You stay here. There's no need for you to stir out of this bed ..."

"But I have to go down to the kitchen to ..."

"We had leek *cawl*. We learned how to peel potatoes last night. We will learn something else today, you can be sure. The *cawl* was very nice. There's some left over – we could reheat it for you ... Won't be a tic ..."

"Maybe in the morning, Moc," Gwyneth says. "Not now."

"I can't stay here—"

"Rest now, my dear," Gwyneth insists.

"The house is not a place for a wife to rest," Beti replies. "There's no escaping the work. That's life ..."

"You'll have to leave it, or there'll be no life left in you," Gwyneth says.

"We leave our work underground," Moc says. "But there's no underground for you to leave. Your work is a constant roundabout. There's enough spare hands here now with the strike and everything. And that's why this strike is happening, isn't it, to get a better life for us."

"But the baby, Moc," Beti says. "We've always said we wanted children to help us when we're too old to work ourselves."

"We need the children now, Beti. And they know that."

"Llew ...?" Beti says. "I must go to the hospital to—"

"Alun and Guto will go morning and night. Don't excite yourself now."

"And how is Llew?"

"He's no worse."

Beti looks at the ring on her little finger.

"Where did this come from? I don't remember ..."

Eira arrives with tea for the four of them.

"Oh yes, I remember now," Beti says.

Chapter 22

A police officer steps away from the massed ranks that guard one of the bridges leading to the Llwynypia mine. Guto notes the three stripes on his arm. As he strides towards them, his bushy moustache and thick eyebrows make him look angrier and more threatening with every step. He even makes Alun look rather small, thinks Guto. The policeman pulls his truncheon from its leather case hanging from his belt when he is within five steps, and waves it in Alun's face. The two of them stand stock still.

"Fed spies, are you?" he says in a loud deep voice.

Neither Alun nor Guto says a word.

"Which pit do you work in?" the sergeant asks.

"There's a strike going on here," Alun says breezily. "Maybe you've heard about it?"

"Don't you try and be clever with me, collier! Which pit?"

"The Pandy."

"Tonypandy, is it? They say that's the breeding ground for every disturbance in the Rhondda! What are you doing up here by the Glamorgan pit in Llwynypia, then?"

"My brother—"

"Looking for some opportunity to create trouble, is it? I've noticed you two. You're back and forth twice a day and you're drinking everything in. Are you spies? You're planning an assault on the Glamorgan, aren't you?"

"Listen—" Alun starts.

"No, you listen to me, you vermin!" The sergeant brandishes his truncheon under Alun's nose. "Do you want to feel the weight of this on your back? D'you know how many truncheons we've got? Tons. A special train from Cardiff has been up, loaded with truncheons. So none of your nonsense. Understand? Or …"

And with that, the sergeant suddenly raises his arm as if he were going to crack the truncheon down on Alun's head. Alun opens his hands and holds them in front of his face.

"We're not here to attack you," he says quietly. "You see the water jack this young lad is carrying? It's *cawl* for his brother, who's up in the hospital on Tyntyla Road."

The sergeant lowers his truncheon. His face relaxes.

"He's poorly, is he?"

Guto nods.

"In the Sanatorium?" the sergeant continues. "Then he must be very ill. We had a place like that not far from my home when I was a child."

"Where are you from, then?" Alun asks.

"Near Swansea. I lost a little sister in the Sanatorium years ago. What's the matter with your brother?"

"Diphtheria."

The sergeant swallows hard.

"Run along to him, before that soup gets cold. And the best of luck to him!"

The policeman turns smartly and walks back to the ranks of dark coats.

As he walks on towards Tyntyla Hospital, Guto looks at

the smoke rising from the chimneys of the powerhouse at the Glamorgan's pithead.

"The fires are still burning at the pithead," he says to Alun.

"Yes. The turbines are still producing electricity to run the pumps."

"But who's stoking the fires? There's over four thousand workers on strike in this pit too, aren't there?"

Alun dawdles, looking across at the Glamorgan site for a long time as he crosses the railway bridge. It's enormous. Eight tall brick chimneys rise from the site. At the heads of the two shafts stand two pairs of winding wheels. Hundreds of wagons stand on their rails – some empty, some full of coal and some full of waste brought up from the earth. He sees the enormous powerhouse and the electricity poles carrying the energy to workshops and offices. This is a true stronghold of industry. The mine's waste tip rises like a mountain from the valley floor. There is dust and ash everywhere and the waters of the Rhondda river, flowing between the pit and the road, run black.

"There's over twenty thousand on strike by now," Alun says. "This is a battle for the rights of the people of these valleys to have a better life for their families. We have to have wages above the poverty wages we see every day. And the colliers of Aberdare, Cwmtillery, Merthyr and Abergwynfi have taken their tools home. It's bound to bring pressure to bear on the works owners."

"But they're still refusing to meet the Fed to discuss pay?"

"That's what we heard yesterday – their final offer is on the table, they say. They are not going to compromise further."

"The devils! But the miners are resolute too."

"You've heard the talk in Tonypandy. There's not many angels around the place, I can tell you that for nothing, Guto."

"But someone's working in the Glamorgan, with all the fires going like that."

"The rumour that's going round is that the owners are bringing labour up here from the docks at Cardiff and Barry. There's enough poverty there, too. The story is that they lie down in the bottom of the empty coal wagons that are coming back into the Glamorgan pit and are then being sneaked into the works along the railway."

"The blacklegs have arrived, then!" Guto says in amazement.

"And the police are a wall of uniforms between the miners and what's happening inside."

"And if there's enough of them to run the powerhouse, maybe they're underground too, cutting coal?"

"It's difficult to say what's happening. You see this high wooden fence along the side of the road, Guto? It's bound to be hiding something from our prying eyes."

"But we didn't see any miners picketing the entrance to the Glamorgan this morning, Alun."

"They tried that first thing yesterday – the policemen told the six who were heading for the pit to picket to turn round and head back home. They said they have no right now to picket."

"And did they listen to them?"

"Of course not! We're not mice in this valley, Guto! 'We're going on to picket peacefully,' they said. And then the policemen took out their truncheons and hit every head and arm that they could get to and forced them back."

"So the policemen are helping the owners, keeping the miners away and letting the blacklegs in through the back door."

"You've got it, Guto!"

They go on to the hospital in silence. As they enter through the doors of the ward and go towards the desk to ask for their masks, the nurse looking after Llew approaches them.

"He's sleeping at the moment. He's been awake all night, fighting for breath and coughing. That cough is draining him. You can come and see him, but I can't wake him for you. He needs his sleep to recover his strength a bit."

At Llew's bedside, they can see that the illness is devouring his little face. In place of the rounded cheeks of a little lad his age, there are deep, pasty hollows.

Although Alun and Guto wait for over an hour, there is no sign of him waking. The only thing to do is leave the soup with the nurse and start back for Tonypandy.

As they cross the railway back towards Llwynypia, it's clear that there's been a change in the situation at the mine. They can hear the sound of loud shouting and, as they round the big bend into Llwynypia Road, they see a large crowd of miners – and their wives – blocking the way.

"Has something happened?" Alun asks a woman in the crowd.

"The police – they've stopped us picketing!" she shouts over tumult. "We know that blacklegs have gone in to work underground. There are people living here that are breaking the strike.

"But the police are minding them like they're innocent

little children. The shift'll be over soon and if we can't picket them on the way in, we can tell them what we think of them on the way out."

"All the other pits this company owns is stopped," says an old miner standing nearby. "I've come down from Clydach, I 'ave. I don' need to be ou'side the Cambrian Colliery. Everyone's respectin' the pickets there, they are. Bu' there's some plan bein' 'atched by them masters of the Glamorgan by 'ere. We need to keep an eye on them, we do."

A shout, louder than the general hubbub, emanates from the depths of the crowd. In front of Alun and Guto and the old miner the road is thick with protesters and pickets – children, women, miners – and everyone is standing together.

"There's thousands here!" cries Guto in amazement.

"And everyone's temper is worsening," adds Alun. "There's some nasty pushing and shoving down the road in front of us."

"End of shift," says the old miner. "Givin' them blacklegs a warm welcome, they are."

"There's two lines of policemen pushing through the crowd," Guto says. He has climbed onto a low wall on the village side of the road. Above them, to the right, the terraced housing of the Llwynypia workers looks down on the road, the river and the pit. "And those who've been underground are walking between them!"

"A police escort for those who break the strike!" screams the woman. "These bobbies are policing for those who are already breaking the strike!"

Many in the crowd agree with her. Things are getting heated, thinks Guto. He sees that the two lines of policemen are coming up the road in their direction.

"They're being steered round this road," Alun observes. "There are too many miners down in the Tonypandy and Cwm Clydach direction. It'll be mayhem if these blacklegs head home on the other road. They're slipping them across the river and down the back streets."

"But they have to pass by us first!" yells the woman. "Go to hell, you blacklegs!"

As the procession draws nearer, the pushing and shouting gets wilder and fiercer. By now there about fifty policemen, with their truncheons out in front of them, forcing a path through the protesters. In the middle of this, about twenty blacklegs are being protected.

From his perch on top of the wall, Guto sees half a dozen young miners suddenly rush the police, punching the blacklegs in the face. He sees raised truncheons flailing wildly before being brought down on the miners' heads. Though the shouting, Guto can hear the hollow thwacks as the truncheons hit bodies. It's plain that miners are falling underfoot. Others turn away with blood pouring from their foreheads and down their faces. But others step into the fray, and the procession makes very slow progress towards the railway bridge.

When they eventually pass through the crowd to where Alun and the others are standing, Guto sees the old miner is very agitated.

"You don' keep the peace like this, mun!" he shouts into the face of a policeman who has just hit a protester with his truncheon. "You're nothin' more than a private army for the pit, you are! Shame on you!"

At that, the policeman raises his truncheon once more and strikes the old man with it. He goes down like a sack of potatoes.

"Monster!" shouts the woman, hurling herself at the policeman and trying to gouge his eyes. He pushes her off and hits her with his truncheon before turning in a blind rage and to whack the next nearest person.

That person is Alun. He has caught the woman as she fell back, and is about to get the truncheon across the side of his head for his trouble.

"No!" An arm grabs the policeman's arm from behind. An arm in the sleeve of a policeman's coat. Guto sees three stripes on the sleeve. The sleeve belongs to the sergeant they had seen on the way to the hospital.

He must have had a word in the ear of the policeman because he moves on, cutting a path through the rest of the crowd and leading the blacklegs towards the railway bridge.

The sergeant nods towards the terraces, which is good as instructing Alun and Guto to escape from the crowd. They can weave their way through those streets and make their way back to Tonypandy without having to push through the middle of the unruly crowd in front of the mine.

As they climb the hill towards the houses, Guto can hear the yelling and screaming and name-calling continuing fiercely down the valley. He knows that one of the blacklegs was familiar, and he tries to imagine the face without the black filth of the mine across it. Yes, he remembers. It was George from the Pandy.

Chapter 23

Early the next morning Guto hears their bedroom door open and close. He hears soft footsteps on the stairs. He lies in his bed. He can stretch out in all directions. There is no Llew to share the bed with him.

Things are different in the house. He is amazed at what has happened, and that everyone has accepted the new arrangements totally naturally. There is no tramp of heavy boots on the street, although the miners still rise early to go on picket duty and support the strike. There is no hooter to be heard trumpeting from the pits, although the strikers have their own trumpet. The miners from the brass band walk along the streets from four o'clock in the morning onwards, playing trumpets to call the pickets out together. He knows that his father, Wil and Alun will be called out later that morning and knows they will be going to the gates of the Glamorgan in Llwynypia.

Dicw had called round late the previous night with the latest news. Things had got very out of hand at the Glamorgan around nine o'clock at night when the night shift blacklegs had tried to go into the mine.

"There are hundreds more policemen there now," Dicw reported. "Some on horses. They're shoving the miners back. Then a gang of younger lads got up onto the rough slope between the houses and the entrance. They were chucking bricks and rocks at the bobbies then. But then the policemen hit back and ran after them and truncheons were flying in all directions. It became a proper fight back and forth – they're still at it. There's bodies of them that's been injured lying in the streets. There's even one or two policemen among them. Then another lot pulled some wooden planks out of the wooden fence that hides the works from the road. You could see the office where they hand out the wages then – and that got showered with stones and smashed up."

"It's turning very nasty," Moc had said, on hearing the latest. "Where will it end? Thousands and thousands of miners and their families have had a bellyful. How many policemen will they have to get in to mollycoddle a handful of blacklegs?"

From his bed, Guto can hear the sound of the fire being laid in the kitchen, the sound of coal being carried in and of food being prepared. But there is no singing to be heard these days. It's not his mother who's the first to rise in Number 17 by now. It's Eira.

Gwyneth Out the Way arrives at half past eight to continue her care of Beti. The three miners have left the house by now. Guto knows that the midwife likes to have the place to herself so he asks his sister if she needs anything from the shop that morning.

"Go and fetch a loaf from Wilkins. Tell him to put it on our account."

There's not much of a welcome at the shop for people living in the terraced housing – Guto can sense that in his bones as he walks up to the polished counter.

"A loaf of bread, please. On the account of Number 17, Eleanor Street."

The girl serving reaches a loaf off the shelf behind her, but Wilkins comes over. His face looks as if he's been sucking a lemon.

"For Number 17, is it? You're on strike, aren't you? Running up debts again. Give me the loaf, Gwen."

He takes the loaf and takes it to a chopping board. He cuts the loaf in half with a bread knife.

"Half a loaf is good enough for striking miners," he says, giving one half back to Gwen. He turns on his heel and walks haughtily back to the woman who he had been serving at another counter. Guto sees Wilkins push the other half of the loaf back behind the counter.

"Too much owing – much less shopping. That's how we play it in this shop!"

Guto walks out into the street with half a loaf under his arm.

A few yards on, he stands in front of Goodmans the Pawnbrokers. He's staring at a pair of shiny black shoes in the window. He's seen those somewhere before, he thinks. Then he hears a familiar voice calling from the other side of the street.

"*Buon giorno*, big man! Come in, I've got something here for you ..."

Guto follows Pietro into the cafe. There are only four customers there, each on his own at a different table, as usual. One conversation is going on throughout the cafe – everyone is talking to everyone else, as usual.

"There's more policemen on their way, it's a fact! I heard that himself, Lionel Lindsay – him with the most stripes in the police – he's asked Churchill to send the infantry and the cavalry here."

"Huh! Churchill! He knows the type that's in the army – he was out in Africa with them. They say he used to cry when he saw what the British Army did out there."

"Then again, 'ee's ready to send them 'ere against the miners, 'ee is! The useless so-and-so!" another says.

"It'll be like that Bloody Sunday in Trafalgar Square? You remember? Soldiers with fixed bayonets running into a crowd of protesters and running those long blades into their bodies. They don't think we're flesh and blood like them."

"There's a big miners' meeting at the Athletic this afternoon, Dai Lend Me says. I heard him say that Churchill's holding the cavalry back in Cardiff but he's sending the Metropolitan Police into Tonypandy first. They're coming from London this afternoon."

"Oh, the riot police from London! They say they're worse than bayonets, they are!"

"I'll tell you this, it's quiet on the street today – with all the pubs closed!"

"Elias Davies, 'im of the clothes shop, 'ee's be'ind tha'. 'Ee's on the bench, is'n'ee, an' they 'ave the right to close pubs, they do."

"Does he think it's beer that's creating the trouble in Llwynypia? He doesn't know the half of it!"

"They say that him and the other magistrates have been begging for days for the army to be sent to the streets of

Tonypandy to guard their shops. And there was no trouble then!"

Pietro leads Guto behind the counter.

"No one is drinking cherryade these days, Guto," he says, picking up a bottle off the counter as he passes. "Nobody is drinking much of anything, to be honest. These are hard times for everyone, Guto. Come through to the *cucina*. Come into the kitchen."

In the back, Amadeo, the father, is seated at the big table, reading a book. Emilia is also there.

"*Buon giorno*, Guto," she says genially, but it's clear she's less busy that usual as well.

Guto glances round, but he sees no sign that Nina is about.

Pietro pours the rest of the cherryade into a glass and presents it to Guto.

"Here you are, Guto. You might as well have the *frizzante* drink before the bubbles all leave. The bottle has been open a week, but the children have no money these days. *Saluti*."

"*Iechyd da!*" Guto responds in Welsh. "And thank you very much." Although the drink is rather flat, he appreciates the taste – and the kindly gesture.

"I'll go out the back way," Guto says, and leaves the kitchen.

He walks back towards Eleanor Street. From there he can look down at the back of the police station and the backs of the shops on the main street. He thinks maybe he'll catch a glimpse of Nina taking tea and biscuits into the police station.

There are many more policemen than usual at the back of the station, thinks Guto. There are masses of them outside, drinking tea. Then he sees Nina. One of the policemen has his arm round her shoulders and is laughing loudly as he helps himself to a biscuit from her plate. She smiles at him.

Guto feels his blood boil. Everyone has to earn a living – he understands that. But that arm ... smiling ... He turns away and faces Number 17's black door.

He takes the half loaf into the kitchen. Eira is attempting to put a meal together in the cooking pot.

"Only half a loaf?"

"That's all Wilkins was prepared to give us."

"How was it on the street?"

"Everyone's in poor spirits. The shops are empty of people but full of goods and they're stopping anyone from having anything. The high street shopkeepers all support the pit owners."

"Oh, maybe not everyone?"

"Well, Goodmans the Pawnbroker is pleased we're poor. He's one. And I saw you'd taken your new shoes to him to get more money ..."

"Wanted to get Mam's ring back, I did ..."

"But what's the sense in the thing? Paying money from your wages for them, and then pawning them and paying more on top of that when you want your shoes back!"

"I haven't got any wages any more."

"What d'you mean?"

"I've given up my work. I'm needed here. For Mam. And anyway, I don't want those ugly old shoes back any more."

Just then, Gwyneth comes downstairs, into the kitchen.

"How's Mam now?" Guto asks.

"How d'you think? She thinks of everyone else before herself. She's fretting for the little baby she's lost. She's fretting about the *crwt bach* in the Sanatorium and she's fretting about everyone in the house. She's fretting that the house isn't clean and tidy, and on top of that she's fretting that the clothes haven't been washed and put away tidily. She's being eaten up with fretting. How on earth can she get better in this black hole we're in?"

* * *

Later that day, the front door of Number 17 bursts open and Dicw's head appears round the kitchen door. He's out of breath, having run with a message from Llwynypia.

"Message from Tyntyla Hospital … Someone found me … in the middle of the crowd … I don't know how … There's thousands and thousands there …Moc's had a truncheon across his head and is bleeding badly but Alun's with him. The message is – someone has to go to Llew, urgently. He's asking for you … this might be the last chance …"

"Out!" Gwyneth shouts. "Don't you shout this all over the house. Guto – you go out too. Go up to the Sanatorium and come back to tell us how he is, but whisper it. Things look pretty grim now … I don't want her upstairs to hear any bad news until she's stronger. I'll send your father to follow you up, once he gets home."

Guto follows Dicw out of the house. They go as far as the

bottom of Llwynypia Road together. Guto goes on up through the terraces and round to the hospital. Dicw heads back to where the battle is intensifying.

By the time Guto is making his way home through the upper terraces of Llwynypia it's nine o'clock at night. He has sat for two hours at his Llew's bedside. He can hear the struggle his brother is having, fighting for breath. As there is nothing else that can be done, he starts to tell him stories – reminding him of walks up the hills surrounding the valley and collecting blackberries in the hollows.

After two hours, the nurse comes to the bed.

"He's breathing easier than he was this morning," she says.

His father arrives, accompanied by Alun. They send Guto home to say that the news is better than expected.

By the time he reaches Llwynypia, the battleground has moved further down, away from the mine. From the bottom of Tonypandy towards the pit Guto can see fenceposts, lumps of rock and bricks in the road. In the midst of this debris, dozens of bloodied miners lie. There are also policemen who have lost their helmets lying there, with blood streaming down their faces.

As he approaches Tonypandy, the entire street is filled with shouting. It is deafening. The miners form a rag-tag army, armed with chair legs and the odd metal bar. Some of them have clothes torn to shreds and bloodied heads. But they are roaring wildly at the row of policemen further up the street, in the direction of the Glamorgan pit.

Guto can see that the police are preparing to attack the

miners once more. A closed-up wall of coats, with truncheons waving, rushes forward. But the miners are not going to give any more ground. With a huge cry that tears through the valley, the miners brandish their weapons and run to attack the policemen. Guto sees stones and bricks flying through the air and truncheons and sticks clashing. He hears swearing and groaning and agonised cries.

As thousands rush to face the police, the crowd thins enough for him to make it to Dunraven Street. He walks along and sees an amazing sight.

A butcher's shop – the door has been torn off its hinges and smashed and flung into the street, and Guto sees half a dozen women inside, sharing the meat with whoever is passing by.

"You've not 'ad your supper yet, 'ave you, butty *bach*! 'Ere you are – 'ave a few lamb chops. An' a nice big steak for your mam."

He sees Dicw walking towards him. He's carrying half a lamb, complete, on his shoulder from the butcher's shop at the far end of the street.

"Something to chew on in the *cawl*," he says, "instead of the endless cabbage-water. I'm only going along to get a bunch of carrots to put in the pot with this."

And off he goes like a man doing a good day's work.

After passing half a dozen other shops, Guto reaches Wilkins', and every window is broken. All the food is being hastily loaded into boxes by a group of sickly-looking children. The children of the family from Eleanor Street that were turned out by the bailiffs are in the middle of the gang.

Elias Davies' shop. Who is this? He sees a woman dressed entirely in black. They are all brand new clothes from the shop, so it seems. A long black frock, a black shawl and a black hat with a delicate black veil concealing her face. Then he hears her voice and recognises her.

"Look, I can afford to mourn properly now. You haven't truly had a bereavement until you've dressed in black from head to toe. And I can afford to mourn now, you see ..."

It is as if she is acting in a pantomime in the Empire. It is Dilys Mainwaring.

He goes on through further devastation. There are more young lads with table legs and bits of fencing arriving in the main street and breaking yet more windows. Strewn across the pavements and into the middle of the road are tins of food, posh hats, fruit, and shoes ...

He thinks about Eira's shoes in the window of Goodman the Pawnbroker's ...

He cannot get the image of little Llew in the hospital bed fighting for breath out of his head ...

Nor the almost empty jug on the mantleshelf ...

Nor the children waiting for their *cawl* in the chapel vestry ...

But by the time he reaches the pawnbroker's shop, clutching three bricks, Guto sees that the wily old fox has pulled down the metal shutters to protect his stock.

He spins round. He sees Bertorelli's cafe across the road with its glass door. The only thing he can see in the glass is the policeman's arm round Nina's shoulder. He throws the brick ...

Chapter 24

The crack widens across the glass pane of the door. Through it, the interior of the shop looks like two pieces of a jigsaw joined together. But Guto can see the picture clearly. He can see a face inside looking out at the street. He can see Pietro's eyes, wide in amazement, staring at him.

Guto runs towards the door.

"Pietro! Pietro! I'm sorry!"

But the eyes do nothing but continue to stare coldly at him. He hears a voice behind him.

"It's Welsh Hills pop we can get in 'ere, isn'it? I fancy some pop I do, after the day we've 'ad. We'll finish smashin' the door', will we?"

"No!" Guto turns to face the voice.

Two boys, about ten years old, are standing there, each carrying a mandrel handle. Guto grabs one of the handles and pulls it out of the hands of the lad. Using it as a weapon, he knocks the other handle out of the other boy's hands.

"C'mon, Bryn – le's go down the street. There's easier places than 'ere. Whaddabout Misery Morris' sweet shop?"

The boys disappear into the crowd. More families are coming down from the terraced housing. Some are organised, taking it seriously, and have brought a wheelbarrow with them – the mother pushing it along the main street and a gaggle of children darting in through the windows. They emerge carrying as much food, drink and clothing as they can carry. The high-class and expensive shops of Tonypandy look like fairground stalls that have been blasted by the worst storms possible.

Guto holds his ground in front of Bertorelli's cafe. If anyone comes too close, threatening to throw a stone through the window or smash it with an iron bar, he warns them off with his mandrel handle.

"Do you want to feel this shaft on your head? The Bertorellis are a family who've left poverty like ours to come here. They work hard and have brought a bit of warmth to our high street. We can sit in there all evening with only one cup of coffee. Remember who your friends are. We'll be needing them again ..."

Some withdraw, ashamed. Others see that they're wasting their time when there are over sixty other shops in the street, and move on.

After keeping this up for half an hour, Guto hears a shout from the direction of Llwynypia Road.

"Go home everyone – the Mets are coming! The Mets are coming!"

A loud screech reaches his ears. The crowd at the top of Dunraven Street acts first and, like an ocean wave, the screech gets carried further and further. Guto sees wives and children and miners turn and run. They leave their loads of goods from the shops scattered across the street. The crowd run like rats back to their boltholes, up the hill and into the terraces.

Guto can see the uniforms of the Metropolitan Police

approaching. These are not going forward to attack as a wall across the street, as the police at the Glamorgan Colliery had done. These London police are in formation: two orderly lines, running down the middle of the street, their truncheons thrusting in all directions. They push the crowd before them. If anyone is fool enough to stand their ground, or too slow in moving aside, they get a beating from policemen from the middle of the line. They move swiftly, leaving dozens of bloodied bodies in their wake.

They're getting closer, Guto thinks. He hides the mandrel handle behind his back, so he doesn't look threatening. As the lines pass him, two of the Mets step towards him and one raises his truncheon, aiming at Guto's face.

"Got you, you little Welsh brat! Say goodbye to your good teeth …"

He hears the door of the cafe opening behind him. Then there's a hand on his shoulder and he feels himself being pulled into the safety of the doorway. He hears Pietro's voice.

"No, no *signori*! This brave lad was *protegsere* my property. *Capisci?* Defend – not attack!"

Pietro pulls Guto into the cafe and closes the door in the face of the London policemen. They carry on in pursuit of the other townspeople still in the street.

"Pietro," says Guto in the darkness, as the noise outside recedes, "I'm sorry. I'm so sorry …"

Guto crumples into the nearest chair, puts his elbows on the table and his face in his hands and, howling, lets the tears stream down his face. Before long he feels Pietro's hand on his head.

"The fury of the crowd, Guto ...the heart beats faster ... hot-headed ... no one thinks ... but everyone is so poor ... it's so hard here ... you don't see where you are but you throw ... It was a mistake while you were in a temper, Guto. Nothing more ..."

At that, Emilia and Nina come through from the back of the cafe.

"*Non male*. Not too bad!" says Pietro. "*Grazie molte a Guto! Signore coraggioso!* He was standing in front of the cafe and protecting it. It's only a crack in one pane. It's nothing! A drink to celebrate! A courageous man!"

He pours out cherryade for Nina and Guto and opens a bottle, which was under the counter, and decants a small amount into glasses for himself and Emilia.

"*Saluté*, and thank you, Guto," Nina says.

"The Polizia Metropolitan will be in Tonypandy for weeks, Guto. With enough money for chips, eh? We will get the cart out, shall we? I heard there is a thousand on their way. And soldiers. And cavalry. The place will be full of customers ..."

"And the strike will go on for ages," Guto says.

"It will be long and painful," Pietro says. "What will you do, Guto? Sell expensive chips to the Polizia and the Carbinieri and give out chips in the chapel for free to the children!"

"We can't win if a thousand Mets help the blacklegs to keep the pits open."

"Not today, perhaps," Pietro says. "But some day, maybe. You have to have a big heart, Guto! There's a big heart in the valley, and the people are *coraggioso*. One day the people of the valley will win."

He walks to the door to the street, opens it, and glances up and down Dunraven Street.

"*Mamma mia*, it's like a war here!"

"It is a war, Pietro. A war between us and them ..."

"It's safe for you now, Guto. Home, quickly."

Some of the shop owners are already nailing corrugated iron sheets over the windows of their empty shops as Guto crosses the street and climbs the hill towards Eleanor Street.

As he opens the door to Number 17 he can sense a change in the house. He steps into the kitchen. There, in the fireside chair, is his mother, her feet on a stool and a blanket over her knees and Dewi asleep in her shawl. Eira is beside the fire, ladling out a bowl of warm *cawl* for her. Gwyneth is sitting at the table, measuring Beti's blood pressure.

"Mam!" Guto goes over to her and grasps her hand.

"I'm stronger, Guto. It was high time for me to get up," she says, but her smile is still weak. "Where've you been, *crwt*?"

"Over at the hospital. The nurse say's Llew's breathing's improving. Dad and Alun are with him now."

"Are you alright, then?"

"Yes, Mam – but it's crazy in the street."

"The shops have been smashed in, is that right?"

"There's not one shop left – the goods are all over the road or under the beds up in the terraces all along the valley."

"It'll be bad here after this."

They hear hobnailed boots running madly along the

stones of the lane behind the house.

"Someone's coming along the gully out the back," Beti says. "They're in a hurry, too."

"If the police are chasing him, I'd better go and open the yard door," Guto says, and walks through to the back.

The mad running slows as it gets closer. Guto opens the back door and the door between the yard and the gully and Wil bursts in.

"Quick! Bolt that door and get inside the house," he says.

Guto closes the back door behind them.

They hear more footsteps running up the gully. Five or six sets this time. They slow down.

They go past. Wil doesn't move a muscle until the sound of big feet recedes from the gully.

"The Mets," he explains to his brother.

"Why?" Guto asks.

"Why d'you think?" Wil says, and goes through to the kitchen to the welcome and questions from his mother and sister.

Five minutes later there's a bang on the front door. Part of the frame comes away as someone forces their way in.

Gwyneth stands up from the table and goes out into the passage to meet them. Guto stands behind her. There are three officers from the Met on the front step, one carrying a sledgehammer.

"Wil the Boxer – 'ee lives 'ere, missus, that's what we believe," says the policeman at the front, as he half turns in the doorway to reveal the source of his information.

Behind him, at the bottom of the steps, stands George, the blackleg from the Pandy.

"We're rounding up all the Tonypandy boxers, see. They're all troublemakers and—"

"Out of here!" Gwyneth bellows in a voice that makes even the policeman jump. "They have just lost a child in this house and if you don't want to lose that block you have on your shoulders, get out of here! Out the way!"

These words burst out of her into the face of the police officer from London. As the attack is so unexpected, he takes a step back. The other two have already retreated down the steps. Gwyneth gives her parting shot.

"And I remember you being born, George y Pandy," she yells at the snitch in the street. "You were a spineless wonder then, and you'll always be a spineless wonder! Get your despicable face out of my sight!"

She closes the door, but without closing the latch because the frame there is broken.

Gwyneth had only just returned to the kitchen when the front door opens again.

"*Jiw-jiw!*" says Alun on his way into the house. "Who came in without knocking? Or need I ask? They're smashing doors like matchsticks along these terraces. Just as well I've got my work tools here. I'll sort it out tomorrow."

Moc follows the lodger into the kitchen.

"How was he?" This is the only thing Beti wants to know, her eyes beseeching as she questions her husband.

"Llew *bach*," says Moc, dropping onto a wooden chair. "He's coming through it."

"Oh, thank goodness!" Tears swim in Beti's eyes. "I don't think I could bear to lose another one."

She hugs Dewi tighter in her arms.

"The white crust is drying up and dropping off bit by bit."

"I said what Mam-gu said would do the trick, didn't I?" Alun says.

"We're lucky to have you as our lodger," Beti says.

"Well," Gwyneth says, standing up, "I'm in your way now. I'm going home."

"Wait, Gwyneth!" Beti calls. "We haven't settled your bill. Pass me the jug, Guto ..."

"No, it doesn't matter about that now," Gwyneth says. "You've got enough on your shoulders as a family. I'll send a letter to the Fed. You're on strike here. You've got a serious health worries. I'll do my best to get some money out of the strike fund to help you."

"Oh, Gwyneth ..." Beti is unable to say more.

Alun sees her out. He prods the damage to the frame as he opens the door for the midwife.

"It's not too bad," Gwyneth says.

"No, it's not. A bit of wood and a coat of paint and it'll be as good as new." Alun looks at the door of Number 17. "Maybe there'll be enough in the pot to give the whole door a new coat. We'll see tomorrow."

* * *

That night, Guto lies in his bed. Every so often he can hear the whistle of one of the London police ... A shout, running ...

He can hear the sound of truncheons ... or a window being broken ...

He shuts his eyes and he can see Nina's face. He sees her smile ...

Tonypandy, thinks Guto, what a place. But it's us, the miners, who have made the valley what it is and we'll own it eventually ...

He sees himself pulling off his work shirt in front of the fire, his face black with coal dust and the odd blue scar showing across his back ...He sees that his hands are hard and rough and covered in bloody cuts ...

He sees a crowd in the Empire and the leaders making speeches from the stage, promising that what is to come will be better than what has been ... He sees moonlight on the waste tips ... He sees soldiers on horseback, the tips of their swords slicing through the air towards a crowd of strikers ... He hears someone shouting, "We deserve better than this and we deserve it now!" ... And then, suddenly, he sees himself in the library in the Institute, of all places, reading an account of the strike in the newspapers, before turning to the shelves to look for a book ...

The sound of feet running along the gully at the back of Number 17 is the last thing Guto hears before falling asleep.

Author's note

In August 1911, the strikers from the Cambrian Combine company went back to work in the coal mines, having accepted the offer made by the owners the previous October – two shillings and threepence a ton. Some had been on strike for almost a year. The dispute left damaging social rifts and poverty in Tonypandy, Pen-y-graig, Cwm Clydach and Llwynypia in the central part of the valley of Cwm Rhondda.

In 1851, there were fewer than 2,000 people living in Cwm Rhondda – which includes the valleys of Rhondda Fawr and Rhondda Fach. By 1911 the number had risen to 152,000 – and this in two narrow, steep-sided valleys. This area had the highest population density in the British Isles.

Coal was the only reason for this phenomenal growth. By 1913, the pits of the Rhondda were raising 9.5 million tons of coal per year – a quarter of Glamorganshire's total production. Before the decline of the industry, there were 750 miles of underground tunnels in the 30-mile length of the two Rhondda valleys.

The industry was a dangerous one. Between 1900 and 1910, fifty miners a year were killed at work in Cwm Rhondda. The geology of the coal seams meant that the work of extraction was difficult and expensive. Because the pit owners were trying to squeeze the maximum money from the rock, the south Wales miners received lower wages than those in England and Scotland, and often worked longer hours for it.

However hard and dangerous the work underground, it's a

The Glamorgan Pit, Llwynypia

shocking fact that more young women and children than miners died in the Rhondda. Of the 2,410 deaths in Cwm Rhondda in 1914, half were people under the age of 15. The infant mortality rate in the Rhondda was the highest in the British Isles. The quality and size of the houses, the lack of clean water and adequate sewerage, overcrowded living conditions and poor food meant that infectious diseases spread frequently and quickly through the terraced housing.

Although great wealth was being created in south Wales from raising coal and exporting it through the docks of Cardiff, Penarth, Barry and similar places, the wages of the thousands of workers that swarmed to the coal mines were very unstable. An important turning point came with the formation of a union for the south Wales miners – the South Wales Miners' Federation, 'the Fed' – in 1898. An eight-hour working day was achieved in 1907. The next battle was for a minimum wage, as so many Valleys families were living in poverty. This was the bone of contention that sparked the big Cambrian Combine strike in the Tonypandy area in 1910, when as many as 30,000 miners went on strike. The strike lasted a year, causing starvation and severe poverty for thousands of families.

In the end, the Cambrian strikers lost, but their leaders published an important pamphlet called *The Miners' Next Step* in Tonypandy in 1912, and this led to securing a minimum wage.

The 1910 strike is particularly remembered for the Tonypandy Riots of the night of Tuesday, 8 November. Because hundreds of policemen were called in to defend the pits, the miners saw that law and order was siding with the wealthy

A crowd of miners waiting to go into their meeting at the Empire Theatre, Tonypandy, November 1910

owners and against the poverty-stricken workers.

An extension to the class of people who owned the mines included the thriving shopkeepers in Tonypandy. They were the justices of the peace, the church elders and the chapel deacons, the owners of streets of houses, and their shops enticed families into debt. That is why the miners' families attacked these shops.

By that night, Winston Churchill, the Home Secretary in London, had sent 200 special constables, officers from the Metropolitan Police, and 70 more mounted police on a special train to Tonypandy. A running battle broke out on the streets, between the constables armed with truncheons and the miners. One miner was killed following a blow to the head and another 500 were injured. In addition to this, 80 of the police received injuries.

Churchill sent a further 200 constables to the Rhondda the following day and, by midday on Wednesday, 9 November, his telegram to the commander of troops deployed to deal with the strike – "... move all the cavalry into the district without delay" – was actioned. A squadron of the Hussars appeared in the area, with their guns and bayonets. In all, Churchill sent almost a thousand Metropolitan Police officers to the Valleys, as well as other contingents of soldiers from various regiments. Many remained until early summer 1911. The soldiers and their bayonets were used to threaten and move on the mass protests of the strikers, and there is no doubt that the workers were defeated because Churchill and the government sent in the force of the state against the people of Wales.

Later on, after the riots, Churchill tried to deny that he had sent in soldiers against workers and families in the Rhondda. Nevertheless, the facts are plain – while he was Home Secretary, he sent a thousand Metropolitan Police officers (effectively, the state's riot police), twelve squadrons of cavalry and five companies of other soldiers to the Valleys to crush the miners' strike of 1910–11. This affected the determination of the miners in their battle for a fair wage. Churchill's action is part of a long tradition of using the army to quell the people: Merthyr, 1831 (at least 24 killed by the government's army); Newport, 1839 (20 protesters killed); Mold, 1869 (4 killed during disturbances following a court cases arising from a miners' strike); and Llanelli, 1911 (2 killed during a rail strike, when Churchill sent 600 soldiers to the town). Supporters of the miners' strike of 1984–85 will remember the miners being mocked by the police with "Maggie pays my Mortgage" t-shirts. (Margaret Thatcher was the prime minister at the time.)

The fact that a higher percentage of children in Wales are growing up in poverty than in any of the other nations of the UK suggests that there is no end to this story ... not yet.

Bibliography

Edwards, Huw T., *Tros y Tresi*, Gwasg Gee, 1956, also at
    https://llyfrgell.porth.ac.uk/View.aspx?id=1654~4q~qLPderUN

Edwards, Huw T., *Troi'r Drol*, Gwasg y March Gwyn, 1963, also at
    https://llyfrgell.porth.ac.uk/View.aspx?id=1597~4w~xVCroOiA

Edwards, Huw T., *Hewn from the Rock*, The Western Mail, 1967, which
    is a translation into English of the two volumes of autobiography
    above.

Egan, David, *Coal Society: History of the South Wales Mining
    Valleys,1840–1980*, Gwasg Gomer, 1987.

Egan, David (translated by Rhiannon Ifan), *Y Gymdeithas Lofaol: Hanes
    Cymoedd Glofaol De Cymru 1840–1980*, Gwasg Gomer, 1988.

Evans, G. & Maddox, D., *The Tonypandy Riots 1910–1911*, University of
    Plymouth Press, 2010.

Francis, Hywel & Smith, Dai, *The Fed: A history of the South Wales
    Miners in the Twentieth Century*, University of Wales Press; revised
    edition, 1988.

Hughes, Colin, *Lime, Lemon & Sarsaparilla – The Italian Community in
    South Wales 1881–1945*, Seren, 1995.

Hughes, Vaughan, *Cymru Fawr: Pan oedd Gwlad Fach yn Arwain y Byd*,
    Gwasg Carreg Gwalch, 2014.

Jones, Lewis, *Cwmardy* (novel, Welsh version originally published
    1937) and *We Live* (the same novel, English version originally
    published 1939), Parthian Books, 2006.

Smith, Dai, *In the Frame: Memory in Society 1910 to 2010*, Parthian
    Books, 2013.

White, Carol & Williams, Sian Rhiannon (Eds), *Struggle or Starve:
    Women's Lives in the South Wales Valleys between the Two World
    Wars*, Honno, 2002.

Williams, D.J., *Yn Chwech ar Hugain Oed*, Gwasg Gomer, 1983.

Welsh Historical Novels
– the complete series

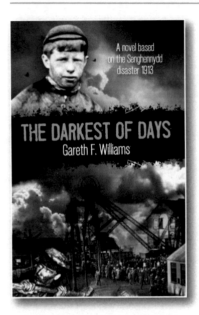

THE DARKEST OF DAYS
Gareth F. Williams

A novel based on the Senghennydd coalmine disaster, 1913

£5.99

Winner of the 2014 Tir na-nOg prize

THE EMPTY ROOM
Angharad Tomos

A Welsh family's fight for a basic human right 1952-1960

£5.99

Shortlisted for the 2015 Tir na-nOg prize

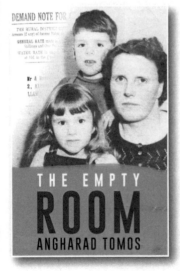

THE IRON DAM
Myrddin ap Dafydd

*A novel full of excitement
and bravery about
ordinary people battling
for their area's future*

£5.99

*Shortlisted for the 2017
Tir na-nOg prize*

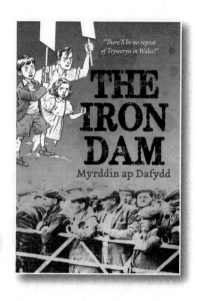

THE MOON IS RED
Myrddin ap Dafydd

*A fire at a Bombing School
in Llŷn in 1936 and the
bombing of the city of
Gernika in the Basque
Country during the
Spanish Civil War – and
one family's story which
ties both events*

£6.99

*Winner of the 2018
Tir na-nOg prize*

UNDER THE WELSH NOT
Myrddin ap Dafydd

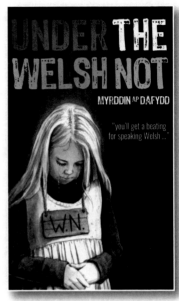

"you'll get a beating for speaking Welsh ..."

Bob starts at Ysgol y Llan at the end of the summer, but he's worried. He doesn't have a word of English. The 'Welsh Not' stigma for speaking Welsh is still used at this school

£7.50

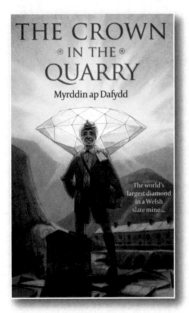

THE CROWN IN THE QUARRY
Myrddin ap Dafydd

The world's largest diamond in a Welsh slate mine in Blaenau Ffestiniog

A novel about evacuees and the story of London's treasures being secretly stored in a slate mine during the Second World War.

£7

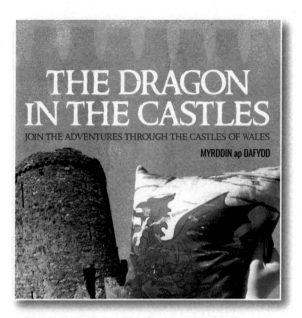

THE DRAGON IN THE CASTLES
Myrddin ap Dafydd

Discover the adventures of the Castles of Wales

The Holiday Blog twins – Gruff and Gwen – are visiting twenty Welsh castles. They come across strange and exciting stories – histories that are sometimes kept out of sight.

Their grandmother has given them an ancient Welsh Dragon flag made into a cushion and this gives them a good excuse to investigate and find the various architectural and historical characteristics of the castles.

All the fun of their finds are presented to you in these Blogs

£7.50